AMIE McCRACKEN

Print Edition
ISBN: 978-3-9820468-2-2
Published by Amie McCracken, 2019

Cover design by Jessica Bell
Cover images from Viktor Tongde, Glebstock, juanmrgt, and.one
Interior design by Amie McCracken
Interior images from vecteezy.com

To my son.

CHAPTER ONE

Summer was on its way, and with it came change and danger. Glimpses of dappled sunlight brought relief and snatches of terror. I pushed thoughts of leaving my mother alone for the summer to the back of my mind and focused on packing for the journey to the ship. The house was abuzz. No one stood still for long, including the dogs. They wandered the rooms, frantic that they would be left behind. I bent down to rub my face on Borno's head. His shivering calmed for that second but started again as soon as I released him and went back to packing.

Mother came into the sleeping room, her tunic covered by a light jacket. She looked thin, though it may have been the loss of her winter coat. Behind her trotted her dog, Bearna. The two dogs were twins, the only two of their litter. Bearna was an auburn golden while Borno was more blond. I didn't have an alert dog of my own. I didn't need one. I didn't over-heat or have uncontrolled seizures. I was different.

I was modified.

"Are you ready, Selah?" Mother danced her fingers over my things.

"I think so. It's not like there's much to pack." I threw my tablet on top of everything else: two sleeping outfits, four training outfits, shoes, lavatory supplies. Everything else for the entire summer would be provided on the ship. Besides having Father nearby, I would have access to food, medicine, and anything I might need to train my body to its limits. I stretched my arms and back, feeling the muscles that had lost some of their strength over the winter. It would be a struggle to reach my peak again.

Mother startled me from my mental checks with a hug. I let the moment wash over me, enveloped in her arms and inhaling her smell of tea and cinnamon. No matter how long she lived in this awful place, she never lost the smell of warmth. Our concrete world couldn't leech that from her.

"Can I have one of your scarves again?" I asked.

She pulled back to look up at me. Our height difference was significant, and I was only seventeen.

"You still need that? At your age?"

I tucked one foot behind the other. It was a childish thing to ask, but I so needed that piece of her to relieve my fear while I was away. I hated leaving her in a city that wasn't safe. When I was younger, I had begged for her to come with us, but there was no room on the ship for anyone who wasn't actively part of the Modification Project. Father was a scientist for the World Health Organization. I was modified and monitored. Mother was simply a civilian.

She reached behind her to the wardrobe and flipped out one of my favorite scarves. It was just the standard gray synthetic material, but it had been used so much that it flowed like water. She wrapped it around her hair and face to make me laugh, then folded it tightly and stuffed it to the bottom of my bag. I prayed the scents would linger in the cloth.

"Let's go! Abira? Selah? Where are the dogs?" Father called from the hall.

Borno bounded from the sleeping room toward Father's voice. Bearna followed at a slower pace. Mother zipped my bag and carried it for me, allowing me one more moment to look around our home. When I met them at the door, they both smiled. Mother's blue eyes shone bright, and I worried the sun would burn so hot through the thin atmosphere that she would go blind. She put on protective glasses, and Father opened the door and reached up to smooth in some cream on Mother's face where she had missed. The entire human population had deteriorated in a harsh climate that didn't have mercy for light skin, hair, and eyes. My darker skin and darker eyes soaked up the light. I turned my face to the sky and smiled.

"I need to go say goodbye to Tobias." Mother nodded, and I skipped over the concrete ground to the house next door.

I walked right in without knocking. "Tobias!"

"In the sitting room," my uncle called back.

My mother wouldn't be completely alone. My father's brother lived next door and engineered new technologies for the cities. He refused to leave his house though. He was never clear about his fear, but my father was very understanding and worked as his liaison with the United Nations. Tobias spent the summers developing new ideas, and in the winter my father presented them to the UN. My uncle was kept out of the loop and always mumbled about the dangers of the system.

His dog ran up to me and sat down. She was a beautiful golden, with silky hair that Tobias brushed every evening.

"Hello Brawn." I patted her head.

The house was identical to ours, made of concrete and mass-manufactured for the entire populace. I found Tobias in the main room at his desk. He didn't take his goggles off or stop soldering. He pointed to a small handheld device on the table.

"That's for you," he said. "Take it with you on the ship."

"What is it?" I picked it up and turned it. It looked like an old-fashioned smartphone, a relic of the old world.

"You can figure it out. Just don't connect it to the standard system. You're smart enough not to do that."

I cocked an eyebrow. I went up to his back and hugged him. He tapped my shoulder twice then went back to work.

"Don't fall on one of your solo climbs, Selah," he said. "I want to see you next winter."

I giggled. "That's the point. I'll see you in a few months."

At the front door, I turned to check if Tobias had followed me. He hadn't, but I smiled anyway and closed the door behind me.

My parents and I walked down the main road with many other families, toward the bus that would take us to the ship. The buildings on either side repeated endlessly. Housing for miles, in a grid, surrounding a common square, all built of concrete. A gray world engineered to protect us from plant and animal life. I saw a few of the modified from my generation and waved. Most didn't wave back. We stood out among the crowd of white-skinned adults like the inverse of bright stars in the night sky. Our olive skin and brown shades of hair didn't belong with our parents. We didn't match.

Reegan ran up to us, turned to smile at me with his perfect smile, and then bent in serious conversation with Father. I blushed, but luckily, my dark skin hid it well.

Mother put an arm around me. "Are you excited for the summer?"

"Excited?"

"You can be excited to see people you haven't seen for months or to spend time training. I know you enjoy stretching your brain, but I also know you get bored over the winter just sitting and reading. You enjoy movement."

"Excited to train, I suppose." I snatched a glance at Reegan. Then the bus rattled up to the square from the other side of the city, and everyone stopped to watch this rusty monstrosity that could disintegrate at any moment. Its only purpose was to transport us to the desert. There would be risk, but the jungle road would be fallow and sleepy for another few weeks. A team of fire-beaters had already gone along the path to kill any growth from the previous fall. The biggest risk would be animals, and they still hadn't figured out how to force their way through metal or concrete.

"Modified and scientists check in and line up here," a woman in a white coat called when she stepped off the bus. The WHO emblem on her breast glowed with cleanliness.

I turned to Mother, forcing tears down my throat.

"Everything will be ok." Her finger traced the one tear I couldn't control. She kissed me on the lips.

I coughed, nodded my head, and took my bag. "I love you."

Father took my hand, kissed Mother, and we stepped into line with Reegan behind us. Father called Borno to him from where he was playing with Bearna.

After we were seated on the bus, I watched my mother through the steel slats over the glass windows. She was compartmentalized, just like my life: winter spent book-learning and chasing away the cold with layers of clothing and chemical fires, summers spent training for a war that threatened us from all sides. I felt so alone in the crowd, leaving my mother to the elements. As we pulled away, she disappeared into the dust cloud long before she would have been lost from sight. I tried to remember the smell of tea and cinnamon rather than the metal tang of the bus and dry dust.

The bus journey was stressful but uneventful. After passing through the city gates and into the jungle, there wasn't much to see but green flashing past. We reached the desert harbor where a large metal structure of stairs and crossbeams led to a plank attached to the ship entrance. The stairs were big, but the ship itself was massive. It glittered in the sunlight, hot metal and glass, resting upon the sand. It wasn't shiny or new. In fact, it was rusty and dented and beaten, beautiful in its own way—an oblong metal egg hovering on the sand using a massive cushion of air and powerful engines. I traced trails leading up the sides over the joists and ledges. It would be an incredible solo climb, if I ever got the chance. I could see exactly how I would do it: near the bow and vertically parallel to a major joist. It would be hot, but the feeling of standing on top would make the scalding worth it. My palms itched at the thought. I flexed my hands.

People started climbing the stairs, and I followed. Burly henchmen flanked the doors and shuttled us in a mob. After everyone was inside, the door slammed and the vacuum sucked the seal tight. In the dark tunnel, I let myself remember the rolling hills of sand, bright sunlight, clouds of dust blown around by the hot wind. I didn't want to be in this metal world. Even concrete was better than this.

The first chamber showered us in decontamination spray. Some people coughed, one dog whimpered. Then the door before us opened, and we shuffled through.

We filed into a large vault, the ten scientists and their dogs heading into an observation room and the modified lining up in formation. Our training leaders, maintenance workers, cooks, maids, and any other crew filed past the scientists into the rest of the ship. As Galon, my generation's assigned leader, walked by, I stretched my neck and smiled. I couldn't be certain, but it looked like he had seen my attempt to catch his eye and deliberately ignored it, turning to talk to the person on the other side.

I noted with surprise that Reegan went with the scientists. He was The First, the initial child of the modified generation. Then came my generation. The generation before Reegan's did exist, but they hadn't survived beyond infancy. Father pulled me aside, hugged me, kissed me, patted me on the head, and smiled.

"You'll be fine," he said. "Chin up. I'll send you a note soon, jitterbug."

"Reuel," one of the other scientists called.

Borno licked my hand. Father called him, and they followed the other scientists and their dogs behind the glass.

Argana, the head of the Modification Project for the WHO, came in and spoke to us, but it was like she spoke to the wall behind us. Her hard eyes never locked on ours. She addressed the room as a whole—there was nothing personal about it. Her dark gray dress stood out among the white coats of the scientists and the light gray tunics of the modified. She was short but imposing with pursed lips and cropped blond hair.

"Welcome to another summer on the ship. We look forward to working with the newest generation and seeing some of the oldest generation moved into other roles. As always, this ship is a small ecosystem in itself. It functions best when everyone is working selflessly for the greater good. Please keep that in mind as you go about your business. Thank you for joining us."

Her thanks fell flat considering we hadn't really chosen this path in life. It had been thrust upon us before we were born. Her heels clapped on the metal floor like gunshots, and another door slammed. In perfect formation, we each moved to a chair and strapped ourselves in. The temperature started to drop. A few kids started shivering, but most sat stock still. I ground my teeth on the mouth guard and locked my tongue in place, like we had been taught, and waited for the electric pulse that would send us into a controlled seizure. A brilliant flash of blue light burst in the room, all the children around me slumped in their chairs in fits.

I was alone.

My eyes found my father's through the glass, seeking explanation for this anomaly. His brows were high. His mouth parted in shock. He violently shook his head at me. The rest of the scientists faced away, watching the screens full of read-outs and information. Before anyone noticed me, I collapsed in my chair to fake my own seizure.

CHAPTER TWO

The only time darkness soothed me was in vast spaces. The holo-studio was exactly that, built as the center of the ship, reaching from floor five all the way through to the top of the ship, with a glass solarceiling. It was an empty room unless the holo was fired up. It could be anything you wished. The holo-studio floor could move to create different terrain, and the atmosphere could be made any version of humid to dry to freezing or hot.

The holos were more than an image. They dissolved into pixels before disappearing, but while they ran, they were as solid as reality. The holo technology had made the training ship possible. Otherwise we would have stayed in the cities under threat of disease and animal attack.

I had lived on this ship the past four summers. It was familiar even if it didn't feel like home. The hum of the engines as we glided through the desert, safe from bacteria and plants and animals, reverberated through the entire ship and buzzed through the metal up into my bones. The desert was another barrier to protect us from the elements, but the ship itself was sealed and traveled on autopilot. It was safe if not comfortable. My feet knew the floor; my back knew the bed; my hands knew the locker where my things were kept. But the holo-studio was somehow different. It was more than home. It was like stepping into the center of my heart.

This morning I woke before the sun. I hadn't done more than doze all night. The absence of a controlled seizure had my nerves crackling. I washed, dressed, and crept from the sleeping room all without waking anyone. I made my way through the maze of metal hallways and staircases to the holo-studio. On the way there, I passed the third turn on floor five and checked to see if I was truly alone, glancing up and down, peering into the dark. The cameras in the ceiling were 360 degrees, but the shadows were deep enough I could slip out of focus when the lights were dim. I reached under a beam to a small lever. It clicked, and a tiny service door slid open next to me. I stepped inside.

It was completely dark, but my eyes soon adjusted enough that I could see there was no note pinned to the wall. What had I been expecting? My father would not have had time in the bustle of unpacking and setting up simulations to come down here and leave a note. But checking gave me a sense of peace. I pressed my ear to the door to detect any footsteps, and hearing none, I slowly opened it. No one was around, so I continued to the holo-studio. It was only a few more turns and a door that slid open for me automatically. Then the darkness of night sky shrouded me, instead of the absence of artificial light suffocating me.

I slipped my shoes off and passed the holo-panel without turning anything on. The room stayed temperate, the sound barrier solid—a cocoon of comfort and darkness. I took my first stance and swept through a series of movements, prepping my body for the pain the next few weeks would bring. This room gave me the space to spread out, to let my mind expand in a way it hadn't all winter long. I stopped thinking while my arms swung in arcs, while my legs pressed deep into the floor and the crown of my head reached to the ceiling and beyond. I worked up a sweat before I really started coming back to myself.

I went to the holo-panel and set up a rock wall on one side, felt the gritty rock and smelled the salt. I craned my head back to look up its sheer face. And then I started climbing. I reached the top in no time, knowing my shoulders wouldn't be happy tomorrow. I went down slowly, letting my muscles settle into their natural rhythm. The floor felt too solid when my feet hit it. I wanted to be in the air again.

I decided to sit for a moment. The others would be arriving soon. I wouldn't be caught in a moment of meditation, but I could afford a few minutes now.

I sat in the middle of the floor, daybreak shining down on me. Certain thoughts flitted around the surface like butterflies: my mother, the seizure, loneliness. I pushed them all aside. I thought of my father and wondered when he would have time to send me a message. He would be busy preparing to test his subjects—the modified—to see if we had changed over the winter. He would have to set the standard baseline for the year.

There was a new generation joining us this year. That made three being tested and two still at home. But Reegan wouldn't be tested this year. He had joined the scientist's ranks. He had been to our house a few times this past winter, which was odd considering travel between the homes was extremely difficult, but he had done it anyway. I had never quite understood why. Until now, realizing his involvement with my father and the science.

A stampede of footsteps alerted me to the arrival of the others. My thoughts danced over the fact that I hadn't had a seizure, but if I was avoiding thoughts of my mother, I was treating thoughts of what happened in the vault like the plague. I jumped to my feet and stepped through a few more poses as the others filed in.

Galon was the last to arrive. He flicked his hand at the holo-panel, and brilliant light flooded the room. I squinted.

My generation was most important right now, because we were more viable than Reegan's generation but more tested than the new generation. There were only nine of us. Galon hated us—me most of all. Our past had not been mended with time, as was evident in his snub of me when we entered the ship. I moved to the far end of the room, next to Henrune and Mag—the nerds of the group—and stayed in formation as we ran through our calisthenics.

But Galon had the freedom to move around the room, while I now had to stick to my spot or incur the wrath of the others in causing chaos. The girls in particular—Reyla, Shirma, and their tag-along Juna—kept tripping me up when Galon faced away. He meandered in my direction, his hands behind his back and a smirk on his chiseled face. I threw myself into the work.

As a team, we crouched and swooped, jumped and heaved. Kellan and Larn shirked the steps when Galon wasn't watching. Reyla giggled with Shirma about something. Geric was a master of the moves. I missed one step, and Galon was on top of me.

"Out of shape after the long winter?" he spat into my face.

"No, sir." I stood ramrod straight.

"Then why are you a step behind?"

"I was distracted, sir."

"Distractions are a personal fault. Three more rounds while the others prepare for the skirmish."

The others marched off to set up the holo and gather the proper weapons. Geric gave me a sad look as he went. We rarely fought each other, only a holographic enemy. And it was all a skirmish, all play, more to test our bodies than to prepare us for anything else. It was a war against time. The world was being overrun, and humans had lost their status.

I rushed through three more rounds and stood panting. Someone thrust a spear at me, and the skirmish began. I ran to keep up with the group, not prepared at all for what might be coming. No one helped me, so I pushed through. We defeated the manic bats and the rogue monkeys, and we trudged our way back through the forest to find Galon sitting on a cushion by the door. He should have been gone already, allowing us to clean up and head to lunch.

"Selah."

Someone in the group giggled, probably Reyla. A hand shoved me forward.

"That was a pathetic display."

I nodded.

"You'll run three more rounds of calisthenics and then see me before you get your lunch."

I hadn't eaten since leaving home yesterday. I was drenched in sweat, even more so than the others, and it was the final straw of my first day. Did he think he could haze me into submission? This was against rules. I was allowed refreshment when I needed it, to keep my body strong.

I stalked forward, let the spear clang to the floor by his feet, and left the room. It would probably affect me later, but I wouldn't take that treatment at the very start of our summer. I headed straight for lunch without even cleaning up. Food would help me clear my head, and then a hot shower was in order.

The food did wonders. The shower was even better, especially since my generation had done things in the opposite order so I had been alone. Just as I finished up dressing, the younger generation came in with scowls on their faces and sweat pouring down their bodies. I smiled, but it didn't garner much reaction.

I went directly to the comms room. If Father hadn't written me yet, perhaps Mother had. I was lucky. A single message blinked on the screen when I logged in. A hologram popped up.

"Hello, Selah." Mother waved. "I thought I might show you around a bit today. You might not remember a lot about the city in the summer, so here is your tour." She turned away and started walking from the house, the camera behind her shoulder. Peering back, she whispered, "Plus this might alleviate some of your fears about my being here alone. I'm not really alone."

She stepped out of the door into the sunshine, immediately bringing her sunglasses down.

"Your uncle is still in his house. I checked on him this morning." She winked at me and walked on.

The city was the same and different. It was still concrete and gray, but now it was more bright and cheery with sunlight shining down and people meandering about. Mother stopped to talk to an old woman about her sewing class later that afternoon. They were both learning better techniques for keeping our clothes tight and snug against the cold but also using better materials in the summer to protect the old from the heat. The manufacturers had developed a new breathable fabric that allowed for less overheating. As mother spoke, the old woman's dog yipped at her. She patted his head and turned to walk back into her cool home. Bearna wasn't worried about Mother, so they continued on.

"That was Mrs. Havert. She's lovely. I worry about her because she has no family left. I wonder what she does all winter. I might ask your father if we can invite her into our home this season, at least for part of it. Though I believe she likes her solitude, like me."

"That's probably why you get along," I whispered.

The hologram was a recording. She couldn't hear me, but I loved to pretend it was real time. No matter how much I pretended—even if I could smell the dust and sunshine and feel my mother's skin as I ran a hand down her arm—it wasn't the real thing.

"Over at the marketplace, they're getting everything ready to go for the growing season. I'll show you how busy it is." She beckoned me with an arm as if I stood right beside her.

The marketplace was crowded and busy already. People set up tables and shouted at each other. Clouds of dust burst into the sky when a tent fell to the concrete ground. My mother skipped through it all like a girl in heaven. She was a recluse at heart, but she enjoyed change, and summer always brought change. Her path wove through the rows of tables that would become stations for sorting and packaging and prepping.

Our entire society subsisted on one type of food, grown in greenhouses and packaged during the summer months to be edible in multiple ways, though it still mostly tasted the same. It was nutrient rich and bland in flavor. The common term was grub, but the UN called it NS. They loved their acronyms—Nutritional Sustenance.

Mother came to a square where children played. There were maybe ten total in a city of hundreds. Birth was regulated, but a few unmodified made it through. Not everyone agreed with the Modification Project. They kept to themselves mostly.

Mother skirted their group, and I heard whispers of "modified" and "nature-killer" and "dangerous." Their whispers were like marshmallows thrown at our skin, but I worried how it made my mother feel to have a daughter and husband both involved in the project while she spent her summers hearing twisted rumors about what we did on the ship.

On the far side of the square was the perimeter wall. In the limited time I had outside between summer and winter, I was constantly there, scaling it with bare fingers and toes. The concrete had a lovely sandstone feel to it and plenty of cracks and crevices that had been poorly repaired over the years. Mother jumped onto the steps leading to the ramparts, climbed the ten stories to the walkway, and made her way along the ledge, forcing the camera to look both ways over the city and across the jungle in the distance. A slight moat of sand stood between the city and the encroaching jungle. Fire-beaters stood above on the wall and below on the sand, fire-blasters armed and ready if anything came beyond the markers of safety. Our world was a small one. The city was one of only five small complexes in the world. Nowhere else did they have modified children. We were the only ones attempting to remedy the demise of our species.

As my mother circled the city in a matter of an hour or so (sped up on the hologram for my benefit), I reminded myself to ask Father why that was so. If the world was attacking us, and our species had stagnated, had stopped evolving, why the UN were letting it happen?

Bearna barked, startling me back to the holo.

"My tour is nearly concluded." Mother stood on a tall parapet at one corner, a beautiful 360-degree view of our green earth, blue sea far in the distance, and a gray, boxed oasis in the center, like a giant target made of stone.

"I love you, Selah." She blew a kiss.

"I love you," I said.

The hologram cut off. The circular room dropped back to dim, the only light from the screen in front of me and four other screens on standby around me. We were allowed to record holos to send back to our families. The room was staged for it, with the equipment required and an empty space in the very center. I went to the middle, sending hand signals to the computer to begin recording.

"Hi Mother."

I stalled.

"I miss you."

Another moment of silence. My mind scrolled through so many options. Did I reassure her? Did I thank her for the tour? Did I react to the things she had shown me?

Did I bring up the non-seizure?

I signaled the camera to stop recording, stepped down, and deleted the file. I would reply later, when I felt more settled, when life was more normal, like she said it would be. I went back to the holo-studio for the second round of training.

CHAPTER THREE

Training was hell, but Galon left me alone for the most part. It seemed odd, considering what I had done earlier, but perhaps he had a more private punishment in mind. He could be sadistic like that.

I decided to check the secret room on the way to bed, and when I found a note there, I had to heed its call, even though every cell in my body screamed for rest. Father had written in our simplest cipher *EMEMTENITEHLBA*. I had no problem meeting him in the lab; the question was whether or not I could be back to the bunks before lights out.

Father's lab was set apart. He was one of the top scientists and had helped found the system that had created the current stream of modification. His predecessor had messed up royally, killed an entire generation with a dangerous gene, and gone crazy because of it.

I ran my fingers along the beams and metal sheets, feeling a little more sprightly and at home. The science level was where I spent my scant extra time, sitting with Father and drinking tea while he shoved his face in a microscope or pulled blood from my arm. He liked to treat me as an extra special test subject. It helped that I didn't mind needles.

I sauntered around the corner into the room and shouted out a hello.

"Hello," Reegan said back to me.

I screeched to a halt. "Oh."

"Hi," he said again.

"Is my father out?"

"I'm right here." He jumped up from behind a counter, his hair in disarray and a cable in his hand. "The lab is a mess this time. They really didn't seal it well enough. There's sand in everything."

I glanced at Reegan and then stepped over to snuggle Borno, who gladly took the cookie I proffered.

"We need to talk." Father was back below the desk, cleaning wires and plugging them in here and there.

Reegan coughed. "Should I step out?"

"No, no. It's fine for you to stay here. Ouch!"

Reegan ducked below the table to check on him. I blushed again. It was impossible to not blush around this rock star. He had been in the news since he was born, only four years before me but enough to make him my senior. The others in his generation had been born just weeks and months after him, but he was The First after the failed attempt.

He had survived and gone on to live a full life, even if he wasn't yet showing signs of naturally evolving. Some of his generation had also been sent to other jobs, but some still trained on the ship so the scientists could keep a close eye on their long-term progress. And now the question was, would I lose the sanctuary of Father's lab to be relegated to the loneliness of the modification levels?

Whatever he wanted to talk about, it must not be the non-seizure, because that would have been dangerous to speak about in front of anyone. I was modified. I was supposed to have seizures when the electrical pulse was set off around me. It was coded in my genes. So why hadn't I? And what did Father want?

I didn't have to wait long.

The table jumped into the air. Father yelled again and then stood, rubbing his head.

"Do you mind finishing that, Reegan?"

"Not a problem." His voice came from below the table, a bit muffled but still sounding like honey.

"Selah."

"Yes?" I fumbled with a set of samples on the other table.

"You walked out of training this morning against your leader's wishes. Galon came directly to me. Why would he do that?"

I was shocked. Galon had tattled. My father had nothing to do with my training except as a science project. He was not a father-figure on this ship. He had no authority over me here. What did Galon think he would accomplish by bringing our disagreement to my father?

"What did he say?" I hated that the question came out choked.

"Just that you disobeyed him and didn't finish the tasks he set forth. He told me as if I could discipline you for not following the program. Should I be doing that?"

The sincerity on Father's face brought me back to the moment in the vault when I had stood alone in a room of seizing children.

"No. I'll handle it. He was actually asking me to do things

beyond the normal program. He seemed to think I was being insubordinate."

Reegan snorted beneath the table.

"Well, it's the first day, jitterbug. Let's try not to do that." He patted my hand and ducked back below the table.

I bent down to rub Borno's exposed belly. Father and Reegan had a mess of wires and conduit running up through the floor to their machines. It made about as much sense as a cipher without a code.

"Father?" I said.

"Yes?"

"The other thing?"

His eyes came up to meet mine. They were deep azure pools. The genetic modification changed a lot of things, but I had always wished I had the blue eyes both my mother and father had. They were a flaw, something that couldn't survive in this harsh environment, but I wanted so badly to be like them, to be *of* them.

"I'll take a scan."

Reegan stopped plugging in wires and looked between the two of us. I walked over to the scanner, and Father came to run it over my body.

"I'm sure it's nothing," he said. "Nothing at all."

The scanner beeped. He nodded and smiled at me. I kissed him on the cheek and turned to leave. Even if the scanner had found anything, I wasn't sure if I wanted to talk about it with Reegan around. I wasn't sure I wanted to talk about it at all.

***

The ship was not set up as a school. We were here to test our bodies and minds based on what we could physically do and what we had learned over winter, but we did continue lessons a few hours a week to make sure we kept learning and to prepare us for future jobs the way the first generation had been trained. Some of the scientists taught us, but mostly we watched teachers on hologram. They were people back in the cities who recorded lessons for us to watch. If we had questions, we had to message them through the standard holo system and wait a few days for a reply. So mostly we didn't ask questions.

"Class, we have talked about this before, but it's incredibly important for you to understand the world we live in today."

Awesome, sociology. A lesson in history and politics and everything else our tiny society was built on. I leaned back in my chair, letting my gaze drift to the ceiling of the student lab. The other students also shifted in their chairs, resulting in creaks and groans and sighs around the room. The holo was recorded, so there was no reprimand from the teacher. We didn't really have to pay attention, but discipline had been ingrained in us since birth. We knew better than to goof off.

"Our society is comprised of five cities spread across the globe. We are run by the UN since the leading governments were wiped out by *Staphylococcus evolutio* thirty-seven years ago. But we are in no way perfect. There are people who follow the rules, there are people who trust the government to protect us, and then there are people who believe the UN isn't protecting us. These are the rebels. You've all seen them. They still take advantage of living in our cities. They have to if they want to survive."

"This is ridiculous," Geric said. "The rebels are a tiny fragment of the population, and they help our economy. Why speak of them this way?"

Shirma reached forward and paused the holo.

"So you think we should just ignore them?" Kellan said. "I think we should wipe them out." He flexed his arms, and the girls next to him giggled.

"Small-minded, that's what you are," Geric said. "If we get rid of them, our population will drop drastically, and then where will we be when we need more people to do the work that needs done?"

"You're contradicting yourself," I spoke up. They all turned as one to look at me. "You said they're just a tiny chunk of the population and then said killing them would ruin us."

"True," Geric conceded. He nodded for far too long as the room sat in silence.

"Maybe we should keep watching the lesson?" Reyla said.

Larn shoved Kellan and coughed. Kellan almost toppled from his seat.

I didn't say anything. Shirma reached forward and restarted the holo. The teacher droned on about the rebels and what they were capable of and how we should keep an eye on them. It felt like a police state when he talked like this. We were told to go to the authorities if our neighbors grew plants in their backyards. Personally I would just burn their plants and let them continue living in ignorance.

"The rebels have a belief system. They think that the SE bacteria and The Thinning were meant to be. They believe humans should fall out of existence because that's nature's plan. We shouldn't be messing with the human genome attempting to rectify the issue. We should let it happen as it needs to happen. What do you all think?"

The holo dissolved into pixels. The room should have burst into chatter, but it was quiet, barring a giggle here and a chair squeak there. I picked at my fingernails, waiting for the others to either speak or start filing out of the room. They did neither, and we all sat there for another agonizing minute. Then I stood and walked out.

After dinner I went to the observation deck. A few people milled around and spoke in whispered conversations. The sun was setting to the left of the ship. The sky seared a beautiful purple as darkness fell. There was just enough light to see to the ceiling and few enough people to be able to ignore their presence, that I reached up to a handhold on a joist by the window and swung myself up. I slipped my shoes off and put my foot against the glass. As the light faded, I pushed myself to climb to the apex. It was hard fighting against gravity, but I was also in my element and forgot what was happening as my hands and feet found their places and pushed on. There was a spot near the ceiling where the joist was level enough I could sit on it.

I got that far and dangled my legs below me. The room emptied of the few people who were left. The stars came out and sparkled their brightest. The observation deck had no artificial lights. I would be alone. Clouds danced across the sky, hazing the sparkles here and there. A bright star, probably a planet, shone near the horizon. The sky glittered unhindered by light pollution because only a few cities across the globe still survived. The moon started to rise, breaking the horizon with its brilliant white light, a beacon to the lonely.

I plotted my course down by the light of the moon, but waited to begin. Voices. Angry voices.

"You don't understand, Argana."

Exactly who I wanted to see. I pulled my legs up to hide in the shadow of the joist.

"I understand completely. You're attempting experiments without laying out what they are ahead of time. You're performing tests in secret," she said.

"I am doing no such thing," my father said. "I am conducting experiments that are within the standard set by the WHO."

The patter of dog feet came into the room. I looked to the stairway and saw Borno. My father and Argana were behind him, silhouetted and ghostly, ringed with light from the stairwell. Borno sniffed his way to my location. He sat under me and tilted his head.

"Please don't bark," I said under my breath.

"They are not new," Father continued. "They're part of the modified project. They're simply in a different direction. We need this, Argana. We're getting nowhere. We need fresh blood."

"I can only make babies as fast as it takes humans to grow them."

"That's not what I'm talking about. I'm talking about new minds, like Reegan's. We need new scientists. People with fresh ideas."

"Again, I can only make humans as fast as they grow. I can't materialize new scientists for you. We've already gathered the best and the brightest."

"Then look again."

"There's nowhere else to look."

"There are—"

"Stop," she interrupted. "This is *not* about new scientists. This is about you keeping secrets from me. I need to know what's going on."

"So you can control it?" Father scoffed.

Borno went back to sniffing and wandering the room, pausing at my shoes. Father walked into the room after him.

"Borno, come." Borno didn't listen.

"Great dog you have there." Argana crossed her arms. "I order you to tell me."

"You're my supervisor, not my queen. I'm within the bounds of my oath. I'll do what I can to make the human race viable again. And sometimes that means not telling everyone everything."

"Oh, I would agree with that at least."

Argana had always scared me. But her easy banter with my father seemed almost playful. Had I read her wrong all along?

"You will have a report for me by next week, or I'll slit your precious dog's throat." Nope, not wrong.

She turned and walked down the stairs. The sound of her heels clacking lasted far longer than I thought it should have. I held my breath, waiting for my father to see my shoes or realize I was tucked above him on a joist at the ceiling.

He didn't. He stood still, watching the moon. Borno went to his side and sat. My father rubbed the dog's head absently.

"This is going to be difficult, Borno. I need to work fast."

My hands were sweaty and started slipping. I took them off the joist one by one and wiped them on my pants.

"I hope my theory is correct. Otherwise Selah's in trouble. We can't let that happen."

He gave the dog a final pat on the head and walked toward the stairway, whistling for Borno to follow.

I really hoped he meant the fact that I hadn't seized, but from overhearing the conversation, my brain was beginning to spiral out of control with ideas. I could be sick. I could have the bacteria. I, and my generation, could be rapidly deteriorating because the modification messed with our cells in a way they couldn't have predicted. I could be on my way to death right now.

My eyes left the skyline and dropped to the floor. It swam underneath me, and vertigo blasted me. I clenched onto the metal and found even less purchase. I forced myself to look up to the moon. It was time to make my way back down to reality.

CHAPTER FOUR

My days were an endless loop of training, eating, showering, sleeping, studying, peeking into the lab and staying if Reegan wasn't around or disappearing back into my own world if he was. One time Borno spotted me before I could escape, so I couldn't leave without at least saying hi. That was mostly all I did. Then I turned about face and fled.

After a week, we had our first baseline check-up. Our bodies were nearly back to decent shape. This year we would be pushed further than ever, but a lot of that stemmed from the fact that no evolution had been recorded yet.

I greeted Father as we filed into the lab, Galon behind me. His finger prodded my back when I stopped to pat Borno. I jumped and skittered away from him. Straight into Reegan, who caught me with both arms and stood strong.

"Sorry," I mumbled.

"You all know the drill," Father said. "Into the isolation tanks please."

We stripped down to our undershirts and shorts, used to near-nude examinations in the presence of each other since birth, and stepped into the tanks onto plastic beds filled with body-encompassing gel. The gel was able to give readings on our vitals as well as keep us comfortable for hours if necessary. Our heads stuck out above, and Reegan came around to close the doors and attach caps with sensors and wires to our heads. When he closed my door, the gel enveloped my body and encased me in warmth. It felt like floating in a pool of water but also being held close in an embrace. I could only assume a womb would feel similar. Reegan tugged the cap over my head. He caught my eye and grinned. I blushed as my brain took me to places it shouldn't go.

Reegan finished fitting my cap, and I followed his gentle hands as he moved on to the next person. My blush read on the monitors as a flash of heat.

Argana stood in the corner of the room with her back straight and her arms crossed. Her gaze looked right through me, and the blush turned ice cold. On either side of her, and also standing by the doors, were men with wide shoulders and black suits. They always patrolled the hallways of the ship and seemed to be both invisible and gigantic.

Father came to put some updates into my tank by plugging in his tablet. "There are a few extra things I want to do with yours, jitterbug."

"What? Why?" I whispered it, terrified the others would notice something was different.

"Just checking. Nothing to worry about. I'll run some extra blood panels on you too."

I couldn't answer. The fear overtook me and shut my mouth for me.

"Selah. Look at me." His face conveyed comfort and strength, none of the fear I myself felt. "You are my daughter.

I want to make sure the winter didn't harm your body more than normal."

"Why would it? And why wouldn't you check the others? Just because I'm your daughter?"

"Yes." He chucked my chin. "And there were higher levels of SE bacteria in the air this winter. The WHO is pushing harder to see results. You are my most promising subject, so not only do I want to ensure that you're healthy because I love you, I also might learn more from you based on what your body is capable of. You've always shown the most aptitude for training and progressing."

I grunted.

The isolation tanks finished their readings and popped the seals, releasing hissing noises as the doors clanged open again. I stayed put and held my arm out for Father to take blood.

The second the needle stabbed my skin, Galon stepped up behind Father and peered over his shoulder.

"That's gruesome," he said.

"Hello Galon," Father said. "Can I help you with something? You know you don't have to escort your group around, and you don't have to stay here for the tests."

"I enjoy taking my role seriously. I don't play favorites." His eyes roved up and down my body. I glared back. "Did you discuss any disciplinary action with *your daughter?*"

Father pulled the needle from my arm and turned to face Galon, blocking me from his view. I leaned over to get a look at Galon's reaction as he took this beating.

"Disciplinary action is not necessary in this situation. In fact, we don't discipline the modified unless they are harming those around them. Or do you not remember the oath you took? This is a peaceful, scientific mission. We are here to monitor as they push their bodies to the limits and train their minds. We are not here to teach them a specific rhetoric or to act in any way that might interfere with the system. In fact, Galon, *my daughter* informed me that you asked her to perform beyond the general protocol."

Galon started to protest, but Father cut him off. "I confirmed this on the video feeds. So if any disciplinary action is necessary, it would be toward you. I'll leave off reporting you since it's the start of the summer. But if it happens again, don't question whether or not I will take action."

Galon's face had gone a paler white than I thought possible. He nodded and stepped back.

"Careful Father. You might force him into a seizure, and then what would we do?"

We didn't talk about why Galon didn't have his own dog. It was rare for someone to not have that kind of protection. I knew why. I wasn't sure if Father did. It was most of why Galon hated the world and hated me.

"He'd survive." Father lined up the needle with a sample container. It bounced off and poked his finger through the glove. "Ouch," he whispered.

I gasped.

"It's ok, Selah. You have nothing contagious. Your modifications won't affect me." He winked.

I gathered my clothes. Reegan had been dealing with the rest of the group and most of them were on their way out to lunch.

"Why are we the only ones fighting the SE?" I tugged a shirt on quickly before Reegan turned around. I wanted to keep Father talking until the room was empty.

"The UN is fighting SE. What do you mean?"

I remembered my father asking Argana for more scientists and her saying there were no more. But was that true?

"Why don't any of the scientists come from other cities? And why aren't any modified children made in the other cities?" I yanked my pants up, hopping to get them all the way up without falling over.

Father set down the tablet he had been looking at. "The UN thought it made more sense to focus the cities on specific tasks. Some provide soldiers and police to fight the forests and keep order. Others provide concrete and materials. It made the most sense to focus the modified where the scientists could work directly with them. No reason to grow children in an environment we can't control or would have to travel long, dangerous distances to visit."

"But we all make grub. We all make clothing."

"Why all the questions, Selah?"

"We learned more about sociology the other day, and I'm worried about Mother with all the rebels that live in our city." I studied my fingernails then tapped them on the table one by one.

Father sighed and leaned against the table, his hand on top of mine to stop the noise. "There is nothing to be worried about. Your mother can take care of herself."

Reegan followed the other students out. We were alone.

"Will you tell me what the results are?" That was my way of asking without asking, *what is possibly wrong with me? Why didn't I have a seizure?*

"Reegan will look at all the results and let you know of any problems, as usual."

"Reegan?" I screeched.

Father raised an eyebrow. "Yes. He's learning the ropes. He has to set all the baselines this year."

"And if there aren't any problems?" I whispered to him.

"Then there are no problems. You won't need to stress. I'm sure you're just fine." He kissed me on the cheek. "Go back to training. You need to sweat it out." His eyes traveled away from mine to land on nothing. The concern I saw there reflected my own, and for just a moment I felt I belonged to this man, that I was truly his. But then a wave of remembrance crashed over me, and I saw myself for what I truly was: a science experiment.

I nodded and nearly ran into Reegan as I rounded the door.

"See you later," he said.

"Yeah, bye," I mumbled, scuttling away.

But I heard them speak and stopped to listen in.

"Reuel?" Reegan said. "Is everything all right?"

I peeked back around the doorway.

"Certainly." Father took the extra blood panel vials and set them on another table behind him. Then he handed his tablet to Reegan. "The results are all on there. Go ahead and get to work."

"And those vials?"

"I'll take care of that. Thanks."

I barely slept that night. The bunk felt made of rocks. The room bombarded me with noises and smells and frustration. The others slept well, which only aggravated the fact that I wasn't sleeping. Yet even though I tossed and turned and spent time thinking, I couldn't organize my thoughts in a coherent manner and deal with the problem at hand.

Concepts and solutions kept evading me. My brain would not shut off, but it also wouldn't focus long enough to make any progress. I finally gave up around sunrise and leapt out of bed, prepared to fight anything that stepped in my path.

I went to the holo-studio and started training, relishing the feel of pushing my muscles to the limit and ignoring my head for a bit.

When the blood pounding in my skull became too much and a headache overwhelmed me, I quit, found some water, and went to the cafeteria.

There I found the usual—three generations of modified eating, three team leaders, two dogs, and a broadcast from the WHO.

With a glass of water and a nutrition bar, I sat down at the end of a nearly empty table to watch.

What I hadn't expected was to see my father and Reegan on the wallscreen.

"We have Dr. Reuel Beechwood and Reegan Powell here, The First modified child who seems to no longer be a child."

Reegan laughed.

"You're giving us a rundown on the latest results from the start of the summer. What can you tell us? What hope can you give us?" The reporter sounded cheery, like he'd had too much stimulant and needed to run it off.

"Everything is going very well so far," Father said. "The first generation, Reegan's group, have started assimilating into normal roles to account for the fact that they have stagnated but also to utilize their well-trained minds in our task."

"Stagnated. You mean they aren't evolving like we hoped they would?"

"No, they're not. But we knew that was a huge possibility

with the first generation. They were an experiment. We have a much better handle on how to control things now. The second generation, one subject in particular, is very promising."

Kellan gave me a sadistic smile. I wondered why he was so obsessed with me, then remembered it was less obsession and more control over his world. He was the ringleader, and I was the odd one out. I didn't fit into his plans, while the others did his bidding. There had been a time when I had tried to join in, but that had backfired majorly, causing a lot of the tension between Galon and I, so I had given up trying.

I smirked back at him and took a big bite of my grub.

"Reegan, you've decided to further the research and testing of your own kind. Is that a noble choice?"

"I'm not sure about noble." He laughed again.

It was his nervous laugh. He had many, and he loved to laugh, but I didn't think I had heard him nervous before. He'd been a celebrity since his birth. This was normal for him. Had he found a passion? Was he that attached to the science to fear losing it or being made fun of?

"I feel called to it. It's important, and I have insight others might not have into the emotional side of enduring this kind of testing. I can relate to the subjects and bring a new perspective." He paused. "I hope."

"That's interesting. Well, we're going to demonstrate on screen how a controlled seizure works with Reegan. The seizures, as you all know, are built into the modified system to be certain that we still have control over their gene structure. How does this work, Dr. Beechwood?"

"We've modified a very specific gene in each and every one of the children. It's a code, almost like a virus in a computer, that allows us to turn a switch off and on. It causes a low-grade seizure where Reegan will convulse and his eyes might roll back in his head. But I assure you he will be fine with the precautions we've taken to protect his body. It is also kept short to minimize the after effects. As most of you know, because of how human bodies function in our harsh world now, the heat of our environment and the loss of pigmentation from our skin has decreased our folate levels. This is why most natural pregnancies end in neural tube defects. In addition our sweat glands cannot cool us sufficiently. This is why many of us have our service dogs to detect a seizure before it occurs.

"Enough of the science lesson on your own body though. I don't need to explain this to you all—you live with it." Father swept at the air in front of his face as if at a fly. He was ever a professor, over-explaining the simplest of things. "You would like to know about the modified. And I'm happy to report that the modified children are producing darker skin, eyes, and hair with each generation to protect them from our decreased atmosphere. They also have stronger sweat glands. But their own seizures are a particular gene mutation created as a control to check if the seizures are from low sweating or from the science. The trigger for the seizure is based on the cooler temperature around their bodies and an electrical pulse. We put these two fail-safes in place so they wouldn't randomly be dropping to the floor in the middle of the day. This is our way of being sure they aren't having seizures the way normal humans are having seizures. The environmental changes have caused an epidemic of massive proportions. Every human is now affected by heat to a staggering degree. So let's show you how Reegan's system works."

Reegan stepped into a glass box after a small chat with Father. He sat in a chair and strapped his arms and legs in while Father strapped his head back and placed a guard in his mouth. I thought I saw a flicker of doubt cross Father's features, but maybe I was just projecting. I forcefully relaxed my leg muscles which had tensed and started bouncing. I was on the edge of my seat. I wanted to go up to the lab where they were, but I knew I wouldn't be allowed in, and I would be too late to see what would happen. Was Reegan going to seize at all? Would he be like me?

Father set some controls on a panel. Reegan began to shiver slightly. Then his little box glowed brilliant blue, and his eyes rolled back.

The microphones were strong. They hadn't picked up Reegan and Father's exchange, but now that Father was back at his desk, his whisper came through like a shout. "You haven't outgrown that?" He rushed to shut the system down and get Reegan out of the box.

"What was that you said, Dr. Beechwood?" The reporter asked. "We didn't quite catch it."

He flipped around to face the cameras. "Oh, nothing. Sorry. I just saw a strange blip on the screen but turns out it was normal. Reegan is again in control of his body, and I just need to get him comfortable. I think we're done here?"

"Yes, thank you for the informative demonstration." The screen went from being split to only showing the reporter. "For now, the WHO is hopeful we'll find a way to continue existing. I'm signing off. We'll have more for you tomorrow."

The screen went black.

The cafeteria bustled on in normalcy. I barely noticed as people starting filing out, as the noise decreased, as someone's footsteps came up behind me.

"Interesting," Galon said.

"What was?" My heart was racing, having not known he was present, or that close, until he spoke. But I studied my nails and breathed deeply.

"What your father said there. He didn't expect Reegan to have a seizure. Isn't that odd? Aren't you all supposed to have seizures?"

I didn't dare look at his face.

"Everyone has seizures," I said. "Including you." I left off the unspoken words. If Galon had a seizure, he probably wouldn't survive it, especially since he no longer had a dog to warn him before it happened. At least my seizures were controlled. Or they were. Now who knew what would happen? Would I have a seizure like a normal human and die from overheating? What if it happened while I was alone?

"Yes, Selah. I can have seizures. We all can. It's the mark of a degrading species that we have fallen so far. But I do believe it's meant to be that way. Perhaps nature is fighting back against your father's science. It's possible that he isn't fixing us at all." His hand brushed my shoulder. "I'll see you in training in ten minutes. Don't be late."

His footsteps faded away before I stood. The blood pooling in my tense legs hit me with dizziness, and I swayed. This wasn't going to be an easy training session. My stress levels were through the roof.

CHAPTER FIVE

It was a strange feeling to be awake when no one else was. Everything was quieter. The world seemed still—paused in its rotation and showing no signs of beginning again—an endless hallway with no doors or sound. While everyone slept, the loneliness crept in. The whole world was asleep. I was the only one conscious. I was isolated.

I swung my feet over the edge of my bunk in the middle of the night. What my father had said to Reegan niggled at me. I wanted to know what he meant. I wanted to know my results. Still in my sleeping tunic, I let my bare feet lead me to the lab. The hallway lights were dim, and the slatted staircase burned the soles of my feet. The tiniest of sounds— a ping, a scuffle, a creak—sent my heart fluttering and my breath into my throat. But I was as alone as I felt.

The lab was dark, and I signaled for the lights. Everything was in its place. My father was not there on one of his midnight binges. I wandered around, touching instruments with my forefinger and trailing my hand on the tables. When I came back to the door, I signaled the lights off and went toward the sleeping rooms. I had been to Father's sleeping room once when he sent me for Borno's water bowl. I remembered which one it was, but I wasn't technically allowed there, especially at night.

I kept my footfalls silent, placing my heels carefully and then letting the rest of my foot glide down to the cold floor. A lock of hair dropped onto my cheek and startled me. I blew it away from my face and whipped my head around to check if someone was behind me. The closer I came to my father's door, the more the adrenaline in my body pumped. I smelled the sharpness of the metal and got the occasional whiff of life as I passed sleeping rooms. The normally gray hallway seemed to be vibrant and glowing. The hairs on my arms stood on end. My senses were on high alert.

I came to my father's door and stood with my nose nearly touching it. Could I hear through it? If I knocked would someone hear, or would Borno bark?

That was when the comfort of night blanketed me. It bolstered my courage instead of making me feel alone and vulnerable. No one would hear. Everyone slept. They were dead to the world.

I lifted my hand and tapped gently with my fingers. Then I danced them across the metal in a random tune. Then I took my knuckles and rapped hard three times. I held my breath and waited—for my father to answer the door, for someone to find me, to know whether or not I should be worried for my father.

The longer I waited, the more I knew something was wrong. And my heart hurt to accept it. I put my back to the wall and slid down until I could cradle my head in my knees. Tears dripped from my eyes to join the silence of a world lost in sleep.

The hologram forest around us dissolved unexpectedly, trees melting into the floor and pine needles puffing away in a blink. We all turned to find Galon standing at the controls with one of the younger generation.

"We've been told to assemble on the observation deck for an announcement."

I clenched my hands on my spear and forced my jaw to relax before I gave myself a headache. The others dropped their spears by the door, almost in glee at having an excuse to pause training. We tramped up to the observation deck, gathering more people as we went.

At the top, Argana stood on a platform while we all filed in and set ourselves in formation. Scientists, crew, and leaders stood behind us. She waited until we were quiet, and even a moment longer until the silence was uncomfortable.

"Thank you for coming today."

I choked on a laugh. Kellan thumped me on the back and threw me a grin. I stepped a millimeter away from him.

Argana began to pace, gesturing with her hands. Her henchmen stood on the floor in front of the stage. Were they there to protect her from us?

"I will get to the point quickly so you can go back to your duties. This ship runs smoothly, but only when the people aboard complete their tasks and work efficiently. It has come to my attention that some people are not doing what they have been tasked with." She stopped to look at the crowd. Her eyes found certain people, boring through them. I wasn't sure if she was pointing out specific people, targeting them with her laser beams, or if she was simply using it as a scare tactic. Whatever was intended, the people around me shuffled and squirmed when her gaze roamed over us. Her eyes found mine for the briefest of moments, and I thought I saw her lip curl, but the feeling was gone as soon as she moved on.

"It has led me to believe that you don't understand the consequences. The human race depends on us. We are the only chance of survival. We are the saviors."

I glanced at my neighbors to see if anyone else thought that was conceited. She had their rapt attention.

"But the reports I've had must mean that you need a demonstration."

I whipped my head back to follow her progress.

"This is what happens to those who don't obey the commands of this ship. We cannot continue in harmony if one note is out of dissonance."

One of her henchmen came from the stairwell, dragging one of the first generation. I let go of a breath I hadn't realized I was holding. My father wasn't the one being punished.

Argana swept her arm to encompass the room and then point grandly to the man being led to her platform.

"This is Mix. He was observed wandering the halls when he shouldn't have been." I gulped. "But beyond that, he also went into the lab and tampered with an experiment." Mix stumbled on the steps and threw his hands out to catch himself, but they were bound together and he crashed at Argana's feet. She bent down to lift him up. "The question is, what were you doing in there, Mix?"

He grunted.

"Speak up please, so everyone can hear," Argana said, her voice sweet and thick.

"Sending information to the rebels."

Argana dropped his arm in disgust and stomped away. "We have no information that would help them, or hinder us. Our mission is to continue the human race. So I can't possibly imagine what you could have sent them that you think would have made a difference. Their cause is misled. They are confused in thinking that we are causing harm, when in fact we are correcting a mistake that will wipe us from this planet. Do you want to be wiped away, Mix? Do you desire destruction?"

"No. But what we do—"

"Thank you. That's all I needed to know. We'll drop you off at the pick-up point. I'm sorry, but there is no guarantee when the UN will arrive to retrieve you."

At this point, the ship ground to a halt, tipping us all dangerously forward. I had never felt the ship stop before, not once in the four years I had been aboard. Two henchmen took Mix by his arms and marched him toward the hatch. It hissed as they opened it and walked with him into the airlock. Mix's eyes as the door closed behind him were wider than the moon. His lips moved, but I couldn't hear him before he was cut off. Whispers passed down from closer to the door, repeating what might have been said.

"Quiet!" Argana said. She hadn't yelled it, but silence fell like a guillotine.

The crowd surged toward the windows so we could watch as the ramp lowered Mix and the henchmen to the ground. A small hut stood in the middle of the desert with a large red X on the roof. The henchmen deposited Mix inside and came out again alone.

"He'll be perfectly comfortable in there," Argana said. "But I want you all to realize that there are only so many drop-off points. They are there for emergencies. We do not always have the ability to stop and get one of you back to the safety of the UN, to their care. This ship is your home. If you follow the rules, we can all be in harmony. Please don't make me do something like this again."

Was that a threat? Had my father in fact been punished already by being dropped off without the shelter of a measly few boards?

The airlock slammed shut, making me jump. Argana left her platform and went to the stairwell. On my other side, a voice slithered into my ear.

"You heard her," Galon said. "One more step out of line and we might have to drop you off in the middle of the desert."

I stepped away from his bad breath and oppressive presence.

"I've done nothing wrong."

"So you say. But I've got a running tally. Watch yourself, Selah, and know that I am as well."

"I wish we could be friends again." I didn't say it very loudly, and Galon almost turned away to leave.

"What did you just say?"

"Nothing. It's nothing." I weaved around him to follow my generation back to the holo-studio. It hurt me that he hated me so much, and yet I couldn't see a way back from where we were. There wasn't an option for finding his forgiveness. That ship had sailed two years ago.

Two years ago, when Galon had confided in me, told me things he hadn't told anyone else. Why a grown man would confide in a young teenager, I hadn't thought about until this moment, but he had, nonetheless. He had told me about his dog. She had been by his side since he was three. They had grown close because he had no siblings. It was most of the reason he and I connected. That and the fact that I didn't fit in with my own kind, the modified, due to being better, stronger, and more important to the study. So I attached myself to our caretaker. Of course that only alienated me further.

Galon's dog was a beautiful golden retriever, just like Borno, with auburn hair and a quiet temperament. She was more than just an alert dog for him. She was a friend, a confidante, beloved. Then he told me how she was caught near the wall one spring, before the fog truly lifted and just as the burn teams were starting up. She dashed off after something in the fog. Galon couldn't see her, but he called for her. A blast of fire erupted in front of him so he couldn't go after her, and when the fog cleared, he saw her charred body lying a few feet from him. He had been so distraught that he hadn't acquired another service dog, preferring to take the risk of seizing and dying in his home all alone.

Galon had told me this story while lying on the floor of the holo-studio, looking up at the stars on a clear night. Three days later, Kellan had coerced the story from me because he told me they wanted to do something special for Galon. They were going to surprise him with a hologram of his dog to keep nearby whenever he was missing her. I wanted to be a part of the crowd, even though I knew something was off, so I jumped at the chance. Kellan had never done anything nice for anyone before, but I wanted to believe the best of him. We were meant to be evolving after all. So I dictated the information, described her in detail, and said I would be happy to deliver the hologram myself.

It was our second year, and I had surpassed so many milestones the year before that I had become a social pariah. It was gradual but harsh. Settling in the first few days seemed normal, but slowly the people at my table lessened until it was only Geric and me. Soon even he left to eat with the others. I was shunned for being in the lead with all medical and physical tests. I had also made friends with Galon and was seen as a teacher's pet.

This particular day broke and felt broken from the start. It was purely a feeling, like nails on a chalkboard or the crick in your neck that you know will burn for hours. It was just one of those days. On that gray morning, surrounded by the ship's steel and concrete, I felt heavy. Something wasn't right. I knew it in my heart.

I pulled myself from bed and looked around the sleeping room. The others were waking and rubbing faces or getting dressed. Everyone was in their place. It was all proper. But a filter over the whole scene made it hazy. Maybe I was having a migraine. I decided to go see Father before breakfast to get medicine.

I looked across the beds to Kellan and smiled. His face stared back. He walked over to hand me the hologram but didn't say anything. I had lost my scant grasp on being included. But what had I done wrong?

The room emptied before I realized I was still sitting in bed under the coarse blanket. I swung my legs over and touched my feet to the cold concrete. It was an instant jolt to my system, but it still didn't set things right. I washed, dressed, and braided my hair. Then I headed into the maze of corridors to find my way to the leaders' room.

One turn. Then another.

The door was ajar, so I hit the button to start the hologram ahead of me. A dog materialized and bounded into the room. Before I crossed the threshold, a scream rent the air. I jerked my head up. Inside the room I found a pool of blood. Beyond that was a large stake and a dog split upon it. A beautiful auburn-haired golden. Even farther I saw Galon, kneeling and weeping. He raised his eyes at my footsteps. I walked carefully around the puddle to his side, my hand outstretched.

"Don't touch me!" He scrambled away. "How could you be so sick?"

I stopped.

"I didn't do this," I whispered.

"You're the only one who knows about her. This won't go unpunished." He stood and strode away.

I dropped my arm by my side and looked down at the blood that separated into pixels around my feet as the hologram dissolved.

I had tried, more than once, to explain. The harder I tried, the more Galon drew away from me. Soon he was answering my pleas for forgiveness with platitudes about nature and how she would seek her vengeance on us. He never once allowed me to explain, and I gave up trying.

And now, even now, he seemed to hate me even more. There was nothing I could do to bring his friendship back.

Spending two hours in the holo-studio beyond the end of training was probably not the best of ideas. My body wasn't singing my praises, but my brain sure felt like mush. It was exactly what I needed to get through the night. I hadn't slept for three nights straight. Father hadn't left notes, he hadn't been in his lab, and it was pushing me to the brink. As I lay in the holo-studio with the lights out, the sky turned from a dusky red to an ominous green. Clouds rolled in, and sand blew across the glass. An alarm sounded, and steel plates slid shut over the glass. A sandstorm. The ship usually traveled at a nominal pace and with few bumps, but during a storm the entire ship was encased in steel for protection and slowed to a crawl. Even with minimal movement, we would feel the power and turbulence of the wind.

Being alone was one thing, being sealed in a metal box was another. I had so hoped for a good night's sleep, but now I knew it wouldn't come. My brain was wired again.

I came to the secret room, and no one was in the hall, so I side-stepped behind a beam and reached down for the lever. From inside the room, I could hear the whistling wind buffeting the ship, searching for cracks and ways in, fingers scrabbling for purchase on a frictionless surface. There were no notes.

I took out my uncle's device, which I had hidden there the first day on the ship while unpacking, and turned it on. The thing blinked to life with a standard 2D screen. It looked like he had left me three choices of app. One was for drawing pictures, one was for puzzles, and one was for typing messages.

Sandstorm coming in. Let's see if this thing does what it's meant to do. You really think I won't need the standard satellite hook-up to get a message to you?

I sent it and waited a few minutes. When nothing came back, I turned it off and left. My uncle was crazy, but he was also a good man. It would have been nice to have that contact with him during these lonely months, but messages from my mother would have to do.

In the comms room, once logged in, I was rewarded with one blinking light. There was a message.

"Selah, my darling, how are you?"

Mother sat in our home, Bearna at her side and a mug of tea steaming on the table.

"I've not been able to reach your father, and it's worrying me. Normally I wouldn't say anything. I don't want to interrupt your intense training. I know how you worry, how you stress. And I don't want to add to that. Yet this seems different somehow. There are times when he gets lost in his research, and I allow him time to be. This doesn't feel the same. There was that broadcast and then nothing. Has he had a breakthrough? I would expect him to tell me so if he had. It just doesn't feel right."

Bearna whined and licked my mother, a sign that she should lower her blood pressure, calm her nerves. I wanted to stroke her cheek.

"Well, hopefully you get this message and you can answer me and say that he's been knee-deep in some new development. I do hope your training is going well. I do love you so."

She didn't even wave. She just clicked the button to end the recording. As the pixels disintegrated, my mother picked up a small device that looked just like the one my uncle had given me. But why would she have that? I had to ignore it though. If I were to get a message out to her before the storm worsened, it would have to happen now.

The ship was connected with the city via satellite, but it was visual. The storm would delay my message to her, if it didn't get lost completely. I stood in the center of the room and gestured for the recording to begin.

"Mother. I don't know what to say other than I don't know

where Father is. I haven't seen him. He hasn't messaged me, and I'm also worried. It doesn't seem right. He doesn't just disappear like this."

I paused and coughed.

"We're in the middle of a sandstorm, so I'm not sure this message will reach you very soon if at all. I love you so very much and wish I was there or you were here or something."

I paused again. Should I mention the device? No. Best not to in case I got a beating from my uncle for it.

"Wishing won't get you anywhere, as you always tell me, so I'll be doing what I can to push myself harder and prove that I'm worth it."

I angrily swiped my hand through the air. The recording backed up and deleted that last sentence.

"Wishing won't get you anywhere, as you always tell me, so I'll be here doing my work and waiting to hear from you. I'll let you know if I hear anything."

I ended the recording and stepped down. The crash of sand on the outside of the ship was overpowering now.

I jogged as I went down the hallway to the bunks. Nearly everyone was asleep, but a few people sat in bed with tablets. I went directly to my locker and reached into the back for the scarf my mother had given me. I yanked it out, wrapped it around my neck, and jumped into bed with my sweaty clothes beginning to solidify and crunch against my skin.

I fell asleep that way, my hair tangled from sweat and the smell of tea and cinnamon blanketing my nose.

***

I sat in the student lab during lunch hour the next day. No one else was there to bother me, and I had the chance to catch up on work. The others would file in soon enough, so I buckled down and focused on studying the karyotype in front of me. I was so absorbed in the work, my vision blurring as I stared at the screen, that I didn't notice someone coming in until they cleared their throat. I whipped around in the chair to face the door, where Argana stood. I gulped.

"I think we need to have a chat," she said.

One of her guards stood by the door as she walked toward me. The other stood outside the door—I could see his sleeve through the window.

"Do your men have names?" I asked, trying to calm my breathing and heart rate. I hadn't seen her since the last round of testing, since before my father disappeared.

"This is Darm, and the other is Trej. Why do you ask?" She sat in a chair across from me, turning to survey the trays of samples sitting on the table there.

"If I'm going to be seeing them often, I should probably be able to say hello. Hi Darm. Nice to meet you."

He nodded and clasped his hands in front of his waist. His shoulders bulged through the suit.

"Any idea where my dad is?" I shouldn't have asked. I really shouldn't have. But it just fell out of my mouth.

"I'm not here to talk about your father. He knows what he needs to do, but I need to be sure that you know your role in all of this."

Her threat on the observation deck had been openly terrifying. Would she really imprison my father?

"My role is to continue training and hopefully begin evolving."

"Yes, Selah. But I want to check up on you. Everything is normal? You're feeling all right?" Her eyebrows creased in concern, almost enough to convince me she actually cared if something was wrong with me. I had let that question slip. I wouldn't bring up my non-seizure. I knew better.

"I'm fine. Why do you ask?"

"We're concerned for all our subjects." She rubbed a finger along one eyebrow.

"I'm a little busy with schoolwork right now. The best thing you can do for me is leave me alone."

"Sure thing." She patted my shoulder and walked away. Just before the door she stopped and looked over her shoulder at me. "I just want to mention that you have a schedule, and activities outside of that schedule should be standard. No roaming up to the labs. No visiting your father's room. Ok?" And then she left.

I blinked a few times, gathered my wits, and waved to Darm. He didn't wave back.

When the door clicked shut, I breathed again. Dizziness threatened to overcome me from the lack of oxygen, but I held onto the desk to keep from tipping over. If I was going to have Argana's attention focused on me, I needed to start being more careful. She was fire, and I was flammable. Other than to find out where my father was, I didn't want anything to do with that witch.

I would be watching doors and the cameras more closely from now on. If she found out I wasn't having controlled seizures, I didn't know what would happen. I would probably end up splayed open on an examination table. I shivered and went back to work, trying to forget the image of my body exposed on a cold metal table, my insides on display, as I lay there alive.

A week later, there was still no news. I felt powerless. I couldn't leave the ship—I couldn't even traverse the other floors without being questioned due to my new famous status of "orphan of missing scientist."

I left another message for Mother. Seeing as she hadn't replied yet, she probably hadn't received the first message due to the storm. While I was in the comms room, the door slammed open. I expected a girl in tears or maybe Galon, who had become increasingly shifty and seemed to be tracking me during my time off. But the person who stood in the light of the hallway was not someone I had anticipated or was ready for. It was Reegan.

He jumped inside the room and shut the door behind him after a furtive glance outside.

"Are the cameras off?" he asked.

The words wouldn't leave my throat, so I nodded.

"You have to come with me." He tugged my sleeve. "Now."

I shut down the station I sat at and followed him from the room. Every corner we passed, he checked both directions for people. His gate was more of a trot than a walk, and I had trouble keeping up without running. When we reached the stairs, he paused to listen for footsteps before climbing to the ninth floor and leading me to my father's lab. Before he opened the door, he turned to face me.

"I'm not sure what happened, but I know this has to be about you. We need to gather what we can and get it out of here. Do you know of anywhere we can hide things on the ship?"

Again, I nodded.

He nodded back and pushed the door open behind him. Over his shoulder the lab was in chaos—tables turned over, screens on their sides and cracked. There was no reason for this mayhem, especially in a world with limited resources. I had been to the lab for the first few days after the broadcast, always stopping by at odd hours, hoping to catch my father in his usual stance—bent over a microscope with a mug of cold tea beside him. He had never been there, but the office had been left alone. Of course I hadn't been back since Argana's threats. Now it was ransacked. For what I wasn't even sure.

Reegan and I stepped inside, careful not to disturb anything that would make loud noise.

He went directly to a bank of hard drives. I went to Father's personal locker, only to find it empty. While Reegan messed around with a tablet and cursed under his breath every few minutes, I lifted furniture back where it belonged. Under a chair in the back corner, I found Borno. He was cowering under a table, shaking uncontrollably. I dove under the table with him, grabbing his scruffy mane and letting the tears that had been bottled up flow. He whimpered.

"What is it?" Reegan whispered from across the room.

I didn't have the breath or the wherewithal to answer. My sob caught in my chest and bellowed out in a guffaw. It was embarrassing, and because of that I couldn't help but release another. Reegan came to my side and bent down next to us, his hand tentatively on my back, light as a feather but present.

"Where could he be?" I finally managed to squeak out.

"Gone" was all Reegan said.

It left so much wanting. Gone as in dead? Gone as in ran

away? Gone as in taken? It wasn't an answer, but it was all we knew.

"That's it? There must be something we can do. There must be."

"I'm sorry, Selah. I think he said something during the public broadcast that has them worried."

"Them?"

"The WHO."

"Do you think they dropped him off in the desert? Was that what the demonstration with Mix was all about?" I twisted my hands into Borno's fur.

"I don't know," he whispered. "I think he's too valuable for that."

So he had to be somewhere on the ship. Even if I couldn't find him, even if it was too dangerous to look and even thinking about searching sent my thoughts to the depths, I could at least be comforted in the idea that he was still in the relative safety of this refuge.

I suddenly realized that I couldn't trust the system. I couldn't trust anyone. Walls erected themselves around me. I closed myself off, slowly but surely. Even Reegan was a risk. So I hooked a hand through Borno's collar and took a deep breath. Without making eye contact, I stood and walked from the room.

"Where are you going to go?"

"Anywhere but here." I kept my back to him. If I looked at him, I would surely break down. His beautiful eyes, his warm smile, they would crumble the walls I was only beginning to build.

"Where will you take Borno? You're not allowed a dog unless he's providing a service. I'm surprised they haven't already taken Borno somewhere."

"I have a place for him." I only hoped he would stay quiet and they weren't watching the cameras too closely. I would have to use crowds instead of walking him around all on my own.

"And your father?"

"What of him?"

Reegan came closer to me. I thought I could feel his breath on my neck, hot and misty. I shuddered.

"We can find him. I took the research from the hard drives. I only copied it, so they won't know I have it. We can find what he found."

Find it and then be punished. Possibly get thrown from the ship to waste away in the desert. Who knows what the UN would do with us once they finally came to get us.

"What if he didn't find anything? We'd be on a wild goose chase for nothing. I need to focus on my training." My heart broke a little at the words. I was denying my father the chance to be found. I was giving up on him.

"Selah."

A few minutes passed, and he didn't say more. I clutched Borno's collar tighter and led him from the room, to the stairwell. Everything suddenly felt tighter, claustrophobic. My world was no longer a mundane science experiment. Now it was a threat around every corner and the chance to get hurt beyond a scratch from a weapon during a skirmish.

I reached the fifth floor and heard footsteps pounding down the stairs behind me.

"Selah. Seriously." Reegan grabbed my shoulder and spun me around. "You can't just leave. We have to *do* something!"

And it was done. I was exposed. The tears came pouring out again.

Reegan took me in his arms, and I sagged into him.

"We'll find him. They can't keep him forever. This isn't a prison ship."

"Isn't it?" I said into his shirt.

"Show me where you're taking Borno."

I nearly blurted it, but my reserved nature won out. "No."

"Ok. Then take him there and come find me in the cafeteria after. We'll figure out what to do."

CHAPTER SIX

My own path felt meandering and almost drunk. Borno was the only thing keeping me standing. I stuck to hallways that had other people to avoid the cameras seeing me alone with Borno. After a trip to the dog-walking room on the science level, I deposited him in the secret room with a blanket, some grub, a water bowl, and a hug. When I left the room, I shut the door and leaned against it just as Galon came around the corner with Kellan trailing him. What a lovely surprise. I banged my head back on the door and cursed the noise it made.

"Why hello," Galon said. "Shouldn't you be in the cafeteria?"

"Just headed there," I said.

"Come on then. No dawdling." Galon prodded me with his claw-like fingers, and Kellan snickered. "You shut up." Galon swung that same hand back and smacked Kellan.

They weren't going to move until I went in front of them, so I gathered my strength and marched forward, keeping a strong pace so there was space left between my back and that pokey hand.

Reegan had mentioned it not being a prison ship, but I certainly felt like a prisoner being marched from my cell to the gallows. Galon's presence was like a shroud, making the claustrophobia even more oppressive. Kellan only added to that feeling with his swagger and gloating. That kid. I had never liked him, but for some reason he was at the top of our pecking order. And because of that, only two years before, when he had offered me that sliver of his friendship, I had grabbed on for dear life. Burn me once, I learn my lesson. Kellan and the others were not, and would never be, my friends. I was alone on this ship.

We entered the cafeteria, and I spotted Reegan. I didn't want to risk questions, so I didn't go to him, instead heading for my normal table without even stopping for food. Galon and Kellan left me there to pick up trays of grub and then joined me at the table. But my avoidance tactic didn't work. Reegan blew my cover.

He walked right over. "Hi."

"Can we help you?" Galon took a big bite and chewed loudly.

"I just need to speak with Selah a moment." He said to me, "Do you want to step out into the hall?"

"You can say what you need to right here. We don't mind," Galon said.

Kellan smirked. I wracked my brains trying to figure out when they had become buddies. Usually Galon didn't like anyone, but then I remembered the smack he had given Kellan earlier.

"Kellan, are you on probation or something? Why aren't you with your cronies?" I said.

That brought on a blush and a flash of anger, but he stayed silent.

"Kellan here is learning the art of respect. He has a knack for ignoring my orders, so we're trying a different approach. He'll be my apprentice for a while, shadowing my every move."

"That sounds fun," I said.

"Anyways," Reegan interrupted, "if I can't take Selah in the hall, can you please vacate the table? I don't think you have the authority to keep her in solitary."

Again the reference to prison. Chills ran down my spine. Was my father really in a cold cell somewhere with only a rock to lay his head on? And without his service dog, his friend.

"Take her in the hall, take her to bed, whatever you need to do my friend. Be my guest." Galon gestured grandly with a sweep of his arm. A tiny smile curved one side of his lips. I felt a flash of both fear and arousal at the mention of being taken to bed. That was quashed by Reegan grabbing my upper arm and dragging me away.

"What the hell?" I ripped my arm away. We went out into the hallway before saying more.

"What's the plan?" he said.

"Plan? My plan is to stay away from everyone, continue my training, and keep my head down. Thanks to you, that'll be a bit more difficult now since Galon was already on my ass and now he'll suspect me of cavorting with you."

"Cavorting?"

"You know what I mean," I mumbled. Apparently I had spent too much time reading novels over the winter. Where had that word come from? 1892?

"Look. I want to find your father. I know you want to find your father. It'll go so much faster if we work together. So what do you say?"

I considered the possibility that Reegan was actually on my side, that he wouldn't turn me over to the WHO for not having seizures. Then a rush of adrenaline hit my system at the idea of even hinting to Reegan I was abnormal. Sweat poured down my back and between my breasts. I squirmed to avoid having to rub the itch away. I couldn't trust him. I couldn't trust anyone. But I did so want to find Father. There had to be a way to use Reegan's information but not reveal my own.

"Ok." I would take it moment by moment and stop things if they went too far.

"Ok. I'll meet you in the cafeteria tomorrow after training. We'll figure out a way to talk then."

He walked away down the corridor and turned into the stairwell. My stomach grumbled, and I remembered Borno, so I went back in to get some grub to go. I used the crowd to hide myself from Galon and Kellan and managed to escape with enough food for both of us.

Borno was immensely grateful to see me, and even more happy that I had brought food. I sat with him in the secret room until I knew everyone would be asleep, and then I made my way to bed, where I knew I would lay awake until dawn when it would all start over again.

I came into training the next morning late, having finally fallen asleep in the dead of night. The giggles from the girls stopped as I entered the room. I glanced at them and then away, glad not to be a part of that but worried I was an involuntary member based on their sudden silence. Galon came in as I started to warm up, Kellan behind him with a scowl on his face. Something told me he didn't enjoy being teacher's pet.

"No skirmishes today. We're running a full simulation."

The group groaned. This meant no lunch, no breaks, a full day of traversing through terrain chosen by Galon to prove our stamina. It was a war instead of a battle. I only hoped he wouldn't choose a water world. Those were the most difficult since the holo-studio was actually capable of filling with water and forcing us to survive on rafts or swim in shark-infested waters.

"We're headed into the jungle. The one surrounding us just now." None of us actually knew what this particular jungle looked like. The ship didn't travel close enough to get more than a fuzzy mirage of green from the observation deck. Some of the kids looked up, possibly hoping for a glimpse of green instead of blue sky.

Galon waved at the controller, and pixels danced before our eyes, swimming around and forming into shapes. A jungle complete with large insects and predators of every kind materialized around us. Someone let out a nervous laugh. I lifted a hand to keep from touching one of the plants.

The terror of a jungle was in the fact that the deadly SE bacteria we feared so much existed on nearly every surface. As far as we knew, the SE bacteria hadn't gone airborne yet. That would be the end of our species. We had been able to survive simply by keeping the animal and plant life at bay. If the SE bacteria started flying through the air and was capable of entering our respiratory systems, it would be a death sentence. Even the modified couldn't risk exposure. We were better at handling our environment, but we weren't immune to the ever-changing, constantly-learning SE bacteria.

It had first been discovered when biologists were researching a pod of dolphins in the Caribbean. Dolphins were intelligent, maybe more so than chimpanzees, and they were fairly docile. This pod attacked the researchers when they got in the water one day. No provocation, just massacre. The only person to survive was the boat operator. He was local, and he ran for his life when the blood started pouring into the ocean around him like a giant stain. He told the story, but almost no one believed him. Until there was news of a panda rescue in China where the pandas revolted. They killed their caretakers quickly and then consumed them slowly.

Stories continued to come from around the globe. From a gorilla preserve in the Congo and a bison farm in North America. Soon it spread from animals to plants. Botanists were getting sick in their labs. Others who cared for greenhouses or botanical gardens were falling ill and being sent to the hospital with mysterious illnesses that all looked similar, though these people had no contact with each other.

By the time the WHO figured out what was going on, it was too late. Whole cities had been razed to the ground. Some countries had been completely wiped out. The UN, WHO, and CDC continued relocating people to safe zones and sending researchers underground to begin finding a solution. The world's population plummeted and then evened out in the hundreds of thousands. Blockades were built. Cities of concrete were raised in a matter of weeks, and we protected ourselves.

When Dr. Morten found that the human race had stopped evolving, it shocked the population. Devolution they called it. Suicides became commonplace. But then his team figured they could try to create designer babies who were more adapted to the environment and, in theory, kick-start our evolution again. The modified were born.

These were all things we hadn't witnessed. We were a generation born after the world went to hell. We had grown up knowing that to touch a plant could be deadly. Beyond that, we had been trained extensively to survive in a world like this. So as the jungle appeared around us, we all took measures to protect our bodies from exposure. We grabbed weapons, steeled our nerves, and set off into the jungle to find whatever challenge Galon would present us with.

We stayed in two small groups, always within hearing distance, creeping through the foliage as if it was made of lasers. With each step I remembered to check the whereabouts of every part of my body, hyper-aware of my surroundings. A leaf fluttered near my forearm, and I moved a millimeter. Any more than that, and I might hit a leaf on the other side. All of these micro-movements were exhausting over time. I had hoped not to get water, but we had ended up in the next worst option.

As we made our way through, the holo-studio constantly sending us in circles with unrecognizable terrain because of the limited space, we heard it. A rustling and a squeal. The leader of each group stopped us until we could ascertain what the threat was. There was no way we could just go rampaging through. We might touch a vine, or a bug might land on our exposed foreheads.

Then it appeared—a boar. But that wasn't all. I tapped

Geric in front of me. He looked back over his shoulder. I nodded a little above and behind the boar. Luckily he saw what I saw and sent the word forward and to the other group. A leopard stood on a branch, hidden by large leaves, except for his glowing eyes.

Signals were sent, plans made, and one group set off to lead the boar away to a safe space where we could dispose of it. The other group stayed to take care of the leopard.

The day went on like this. We paused for water breaks but nothing else. I wondered for a moment how we didn't get dizzy walking in circles that didn't look like circles but certainly felt like them. It was a form of torture, this endless parade.

As we came to the finish, Galon greeted us. He looked fat and happy, lounging against the wall, while I felt like I could touch my spine through my stomach.

We put the weapons away and filed out of the room. Of course Galon pulled me aside. What else was he going to do?

"The gossip is that no one has heard from your father. He must have really messed up this time." His spit hit me on my cheek and ear, but I was made of metal, part of the ship we lived on. Nothing he said would penetrate.

"That's nice, Galon. Can I help you with anything?"

"I just want to say good riddance. Your father was a halfwit. He was never going to find the cure."

"But I thought you didn't want to be cured." I looked him in the eye. I wanted to know what he really thought. I wanted to see into his soul.

"The human race is on a path, and we shouldn't mess with that." His fingers gripped my bicep gently.

"You sound like a radical. That's dangerous."

"In what way? I'll disappear like your father? I think not. I've done my duty. I'll be praised in the end."

"The end of the world? You won't make it there, Galon. Have a nice day." I ripped my arm from his hand.

At this rate, I was going to get a bruise on both arms from so many people grabbing at me. For now all I wanted was a shower. I didn't even want to consider the implications of what Galon had said. I just needed the cleansing clarity of hot water running over me. So I ignored it all and left.

CHAPTER SEVEN

In the cafeteria that evening, I tried my best to ignore thoughts of meeting up with Reegan. It wasn't hard to keep my thoughts at bay, considering the cafeteria was hopping. The two other modified generations were there as well. The leaders and a few scientists sat at a table with their dogs below, sneaking bits of food under as they chatted.

Our all-day battle had made us later than usual. The older generation was quiet and reserved. They were also fewer considering some of them had been placed in positions within the WHO to help further the research. The ones who were still around for training and testing were much more interested in stimulating their brains, so they spent their mealtime discussing differential equations, the possibility of an NS crisis, or the best strategy to use in chess. Would they, or had they already, begun pairing off? They were certainly old enough to be having children of their own. That brought up the question of whether or not the children of the modified would be modified themselves. Would we completely ruin our species by messing with genes and DNA and somehow breeding that mess through? All without actually evolving?

The raucous younger generation pulled me from my train. A few boys ran around, chasing each other for something the leader had yanked from a girl. It was all so adorable—except for the smell as the boys ran by me. I wrinkled my nose. They all needed to learn better hygiene. We had been that way the first year too, until the constant competition had beaten it out of us. Now we were vindictive and angry, though more clean. Hopefully we would soon reach the intellectual stage of the older generation. We sure needed it just like the younger generation needed a bath.

Kellan sat down next to me, chewing loudly. "Hi."

"Hi?"

"I just need to get away from Galon for a second. Ok?"

"Whatever."

A broadcast popped up on the wallscreen. No one really paid attention until one of the WHO guards shouted, and the room quieted. It was an update from the UN.

"This is a standard update to keep all citizens apprised of our situation. The security level is currently set to yellow in all cities. Most species of plants are currently pollinating, so it is advised that you wear respiratory protection and stay inside as much as possible. The burn crews are working day and night to keep the air around the cities clear, but since we haven't been able to implement the glass structures yet, the cities are still exposed by air. Be assured though, the SE bacteria itself is not airborne. We are only worried about any pollen that might be infected."

My mother would stay inside. But I certainly wished I had heard from her. I would send her another message after speaking with Reegan. I might even send one off to my uncle, though I knew he rarely turned on his government-assigned system.

I perused the room in search of Reegan while the broadcast continued.

"The production of food and clothing and other consumables is going well. Reports state that we are right on track to be safely provisioned for winter."

I took a bite of my grub scramble. It was bland, as everything else was. The flavor did nothing to light up my mouth. After years of the same thing over and over, food was nothing special. My mother and father spoke to me of food that burst in your mouth, that made your lips pucker and your eyes water, that slid down your throat, that made you feel sick. Our food now was engineered to use man-made products that our bodies utilized perfectly. There was no food poisoning, but there were no delicacies. There were only nutrients and maybe ten different ways of preparing them. At least it cut down on decision-making.

The reporter's voice pulled me back to the room when I heard the words "Modified Project."

"Results are looking up. The scientists on the WHO Modified Project ship, coasting through the desert as I speak, are working through the night because they believe they have finally created something that will force a breakthrough. The system has continuously been perfected over the years, and with a third generation of modified children now being tested, it's possible that we might see results within a generation or two. To some that might sound like a long time, but for the science it's mere minutes."

Only if you looked at evolution from Darwin's standpoint. That guy was an idiot. I couldn't believe they were still using some of his research when they had made leaps and bounds in the past ten years alone. It was like some sappy religion, this belief in Darwin's theories. Of course he had been a genius. But that was then. Now we knew so much more.

Reegan sat down next to me. I jumped.

"Sorry," he said.

"No problem. Was just thinking."

"About what?"

"Darwin."

"That idiot?"

I laughed.

"What? What did I say?" Reegan laughed reactively, but then it continued on beyond my laugh and became his own.

"You only spoke my thoughts aloud."

"Well, that *is* funny."

Kellan had left the table while I was wandering through my brain, but Galon was on his way over. It was like I had another sense built specifically for him. The hairs on the back of my neck stood up, and I spotted him across the room, eyes trained on me.

"Let's get out of here," I said to Reegan.

We both stood and booked it through the crowd, putting as much distance and as many obstacles between us and Galon as possible.

***

I led Reegan to the secret room. Borno was giddy when we appeared. I quieted him but then had to turn and quiet Reegan. He couldn't stop exclaiming over this hidden space.

"How did this fall through the plans? Every room on this ship is intended for something incredibly specific. How did they let this happen?"

"Things happen." I shrugged. "Be quiet. The door isn't sound proof."

He turned in circles, searching the ceiling and the walls.

"What are you looking for?" I asked.

Borno scarfed down what food I had brought him. Then he splattered me with water while he drank sloppily from a cup. I'd have to sneak him to the dog-walking room on level four after we talked.

"The mistake. It looks like this is built into the curve of the wall, so someone just added it in for fun. I wonder if it exists on other floors."

"It doesn't."

I must have been too harsh with my tone. He stopped his awestruck moment to look me in the face.

"Sorry," I said.

"You sound pretty bitter about it."

"Not bitter. I've had a lot of time to search the ship."

"On other floors?"

"In previous years I got away with it because I could play dumb if anyone caught me. The past two years I haven't been able to do it as much, but honestly I know this ship like the back of my hand, so I don't need to explore anymore."

"And the cameras? You never got in trouble?"

"Those are avoidable."

Reegan snorted. "Excellent." He bent down in front of me and patted Borno. "Then you'll know if there are holding cells where they could keep your father."

"Of course there are. Do you think they're idiots? This is a self-contained city. They needed some sort of prison. It's on the lowest level behind the boilers and engines. There's no visible access and nothing on the blueprints. I know the rooms are there, but I've never seen them."

"Oh."

"So I guess we're done then." I wiped my hands on my pants and turned to the door.

"Wait. That's it? Really?"

"Reegan." I took a deep breath. "I can't do this. What's done is done, and I think we should just move on."

"You're ok with what they did? You're just going to be complacent about it?"

"I have no control over my life. I'm a science experiment. What do you expect me to do?"

He yanked me around by my shoulder and nearly shouted at me. "Take control!"

"Hush!" I peeked over my shoulder as if I could see through walls. Borno didn't seem alarmed, so hopefully there was no one standing on the other side wondering at the conversation seemingly coming from the outside of the ship.

"This is your life. No matter how much you belong to the science, you are still a human being with human rights. It's stated in our contracts."

"Contracts. We have contracts. Doesn't that seem odd to you? I have a contract to allow me to live." I rubbed my shoulder.

"We have contracts to protect ourselves from the system. We work for them, just like any employee."

"Where's my compensation?"

He laughed, a bark of a laugh like I would expect from one of the dogs.

"Seriously, can you not quiet down?"

"I'll be quiet when you agree to help me find your father." Then he proceeded to belt out an old lullaby at the top of his voice, waving his arms and stomping with the beat.

"Stop!" I whispered.

Borno was getting agitated as well, but that was probably due to Reegan's off-key singing.

I grabbed his arms, a little too hard—but he was due a bruise or two in payback for the times he had grabbed me—and yanked them down to his sides.

"Well?" he said.

An idea came to me. A way to prove Reegan's trustworthiness.

"I'll pass you a note tomorrow. If you can answer me in kind, then I'll help you."

His eyebrows raised.

"That's as much as you're getting for now," I said. Then I realized I still held his arms, his strong and muscled arms. I blushed and dropped my hands.

He laughed again, but this time quietly, and I listened at the door for passing footsteps so I could escape this tiny room filled with so much intensity.

I passed Reegan the note at lunch, not really sure if I wanted him to be able to decipher it or not. To understand my note, he would have to have been wholly trusted by my father. It was his personal cipher, one he hadn't taught me until I was well into my teen years, and he had not only tested me with simpler ciphers since childhood but also trusted me enough to know that I would be able to read his most private notes. My mother knew it, but she wasn't a wiz at ciphers, so to decode something took her a long while. At this point, I could read the cipher as if it were written in plain English.

I didn't stick around to find out if he could read the note. I went straight to the comms room to attempt another message to my mother. Something in me broke and gave way like a dam before a storm when I logged in and saw the blinking light for an incoming message. It was my mother, though it was only typed out. *I love you. All is ok here.*

I could have read into that. I could have stressed myself further. But instead I let go and gave in to the emotion. I then recorded a long message back to her about my mundane days and what this summer had been like so far aboard the ship. I went into minute detail about the battle the other day. I gave her a glimpse of my world like she had hers just a few weeks before.

As I signed off, Reegan walked into the room.

"You know there's a recording light outside the door, right?" I went to the screen and erased what I had just said, editing the hologram to end just before. I sent it off.

"Green."

"The rules were that you answer me in kind. Can you write the cipher?" I put my hands on my hips, waiting for his response. He immediately pulled out a tablet and opened the note app. He scribbled something with his finger on the screen and held it up to face me.

$$x_{42} = \frac{\varphi^{42} - (1-\varphi)^{42}}{\sqrt{5}}$$

znswv

I solved the math equation to get the key for the Vigenère cipher and then read it. "Interesting choice for a favorite color." The color of plants, of growing things. "Ok, fine. What do you want me to do?"

Reegan laughed. I didn't think I would ever get sick of the

way he threw his head back and let that joyous sound come from the deep. "I'm glad we're on the same page now. The first thing is to gather everything we know and analyze it," Reegan said.

"You're such a scientist."

"Ha! I know, right? Seems I've found something that really suits me."

"You already pulled from the lab. I don't think there *is* much else, is there?"

"Your father left you notes, right? I never knew you guys had a secret room. I just assumed he put them in your locker. But could there be a note somewhere else?"

"I'll look, but I doubt it. He didn't have a habit of hiding them everywhere. He mostly stuck them in the room, and they mostly covered boring topics. There were never any government secrets passing between us."

"But you can read his personal cipher."

"Yes." It was a long, drawn-out yes. A question within a statement. I sat down in one of the chairs.

"Then he must have trained you for something like this. He's been keeping secrets. Otherwise why the personal cipher? Why something the WHO can't read? Why pass you *paper* notes."

I had never thought of it that way. Paper was precious. Why *had* he used paper instead of just messaging me on my tablet? Now I was theorizing all sorts of conspiracies—a track that would drive me up the wall. I had to stop the fantasies.

"Maybe. I'll look for a note. Don't get your hopes up." I turned to leave.

"Selah, wait. We'll find him, ok?"

It was this moment I would store in my memory banks

forever. The chill in the room, the feel of Reegan's knuckles as he brushed them down my arm, the glint in his eye, the slight smile. I shivered and then bolted.

CHAPTER EIGHT

I was early to the student lab and walked in on the scientist setting up our experiment for the day. He placed Petri dishes at each of the seats, and he wore gloves to do so. His dog sat by the door. A low growl came from his throat as I walked by, and I gave him his space.

"What's inside them?" I plunked down on my chair.

This particular scientist, Dr. Petali, was not a man my father spoke highly of. I had respect for most of his colleagues, but this guy had too much love for Argana. I peered at the dish, holding my breath.

"Bacteria samples. You'll compare them and see if you can find out which one is the deadly SE bacteria that's wiping us out."

I jumped back, wiping my hand on my pants. "Seriously?"

"Seriously." He placed the last dish and removed his gloves. "The gloves are over there, along with goggles. Feel free to get started, though you'll be working together as a group."

Then he went to the screen and brought up the instructions for the day before leaving me alone in the lab. I skipped the gloves and goggled and went straight for a protective suit that covered me completely. Once fully ensconced in gear, I sat down at my chair and waited for the others. I wasn't looking forward to touching the Petri dishes, but I definitely didn't want to do it before anyone else was in the room. They would accuse me of infecting the entire room or something else just as horrible.

People trickled in, still munching on lunch or drinking from their water bottles. Geric sat next to me and leaned over to whisper.

"What's with the getup?"

I jerked my head toward the screen so he could read the instructions. His face turned white and then green before he got up to put his gear on.

"Awesome," Kellan said as he read the screen.

"Do we have to do this?" Reyla asked.

"No," I said. "But I suppose learning about the *Staphylococcus evolutio* will help us battle it."

Reyla blanched and then went to get her gear. Everyone copied me and put on suits as well. Apparently Dr. Petali wasn't as cautious as we were.

We peered at each Petri dish under the microscopes in turn. Each little floater wiggled around in the solution. There were subtle differences to the tiny bubble clusters, but nothing big enough that we could visually determine which bacteria belonged to which label.

"How are we supposed to handle this stuff? They haven't taught us that," Kellan said. "This is such bullshit. They just throw us in a room with the most dangerous disease in the world and tell us to figure it out?"

"These bacteria aren't contagious," I said.

"How could you possibly know that?" Geric said.

"Do you see the purple rings around all of them?"

Geric dipped his head to the microscope again. "No."

"Focus the microscope on the solution, not the bacteria."

He did so.

"Oh," he said. "Is that a barrier?"

"Yep."

Kellan started stripping off the coveralls, and the girls followed suit. The rest of the room copied them, except Geric and I.

"Why are you still dressed?" Shirma asked. She fluffed her hair.

"You trust that barrier?" Geric said.

I snorted.

Geric and I stayed protected while the others worked bare-skinned. We ended up pulling samples of the bacteria into syringes and running them through the DNA splicer to determine their sequence. It was much easier to label the bacteria when we could read their code on a screen. And at that point, Geric and I were able to take off the constricting clothing. I was drenched underneath, and with the chill of the lab came shivering.

"Why don't we have catalogues of all the sequences? That way we could keep up with this crazy stuff," Kellan said.

"It changes," Geric said.

"We do have all of the known versions of the code." I pulled it up on the screen. There seemed to be hundreds of versions, each one more complex than the last.

"Oh," Kellan said. "So in other words, we'll never beat it."

"That's why we're trying to evolve. Curing the bacteria would just create a new strain. They've already tried that." I opened an article from before the modified were born.

Geric nodded and finished cleaning up what he could from the experiment. Kellan didn't even bother reading the article, so I closed everything on the screen and helped Geric.

"I guess Selah is just smarter than all of us." Kellan leaned against the back wall, chatting with some of the others.

They were grouped in a circle, closing themselves off and speaking in low undertones. I glanced at Geric to see his reaction, and his eyes jumped away from mine. I brushed it off, finished my assignment, and sent it to the appropriate scientist. I took my tablet with me when I left the room, and I didn't look back to check if the others needed more help. They could handle themselves. I just hoped they would dispose of the bacteria samples properly. I made a note to check the next time I walked into the lab.

"Selah. Wake up."

Something tickled my nose. I snorted it away and rolled over.

"Selah," a voice teased.

Something tickled my ear. I swatted it away.

"Selah!" the voice screamed. I flew forward and whacked my head on the bunk above. All around my bed stood the others. Kellan held a ribbon.

"Good morning," he said. As if he greeted me every morning with a cup of hot tea ready. As if he was a friend.

"Can I help you?" I rubbed my face and the spot on my head that now ached.

"Just want to warn you that we're due for training in," he pretended to look at the wall for the time, "three minutes or so. See you there!" He waved with the ribbon over his shoulder as the group ran from the room. I peeked at my tablet and confirmed his statement.

"Crap," I muttered.

I jumped from bed and tore my clothes off. I threw on a new set of training clothes and pulled my hair up in a bun. Galon was going to murder me.

I was out of breath by the time I reached the holo-studio. There was a simulation already set up, a forest with pine trees and moss. But I was alone with the birdsong.

I grabbed a weapon from the stash and made my way into the forest. I tried my hardest to be silent, but staying away from the plants meant I couldn't watch every step. My feet found sticks every other time I set them down. The pine needles on the ground quieted my passage, and the packed dirt and moss also helped. But whenever I snapped a stick, I flinched as the noise echoed around me.

The room was only so big, so the others couldn't be far. But after a while of traversing the mountains, I thought to try another tactic. They were obviously tracking me somehow, so I stopped. I found a boulder with sufficient handholds and scaled it. I sat in a crevice near the top, hidden on three sides and covered by a pine tree in front of me. I was incredibly patient, very capable of being silent much longer than any of the others. But it wasn't a waiting game. They knew where I was. As soon as I felt hidden, while still not letting pine needles touch me, an arrow whizzed by my head. It must have been Reyla. She was a terrible shot. Why they would have had her do that...but then I realized why as a spear thunked into the tree next to me. And a stone landed by my feet. And another arrow slipped by my arm, almost near enough to scrape me. They weren't trying to hit me. I sat tight and ignored it all. Gradually their missiles came closer and closer.

Until it stopped. Everything went silent. I had never caught a glimpse of a single person. The lights in the room turned off. The hologram disappeared. Only the boulder I sat on remained to support me. I closed my eyes, trying to calm my heartbeat. When I opened my eyes, it was as if I hadn't. They had closed the metal panels over the solarglass. Who knew how they had hacked the system and made that happen, but it achieved the desired effect.

I couldn't swallow. I couldn't catch a breath. Sweat dripped down my skin. I clenched and unclenched my hands, shaking out my feet as if they were numb. My chest hurt, and I realized I could see something. A tiny pinprick of light in the distance. Hopefully the door or the panel for the hologram system. Something to lead me to safety.

I didn't want to be so alone, so isolated. I knew I didn't belong anywhere, not with the people my age nor with Reegan nor with my family, who I didn't look like and barely shared genetic material with. Was I really their child? Was I really from their DNA if I had been altered as much as I had? Wasn't I more just a creature made by science? Belonging nowhere?

I sat another moment, gathering courage. Then I forced myself to trust my hands. They knew how to do this. I flipped onto my stomach, hugging the boulder tightly, and tapped my toes around below me. One foot found a spot. The other found enough friction against the stone. I lowered my hands to their holds, then felt with my feet, clinging to the rock face with my fingertips. I bit my lip and reminded myself to breathe.

The rock wasn't tall, but in utter darkness it felt like three stories before I reached the floor. I placed my cheek against the rock and let out a long sigh. As soon as my hands left the surface, it too pixelated and disappeared. I then turned to face what was hopefully the door.

I crept toward the light, one foot in front of the other.

It was the hologram panel. I reached up and signaled for the lights. I was alone.

I ran from the room, my beloved holo-studio where I had felt so at home now held this bitter aftertaste. I hoped that would ease with time, but for now I went to my only sanctuary left, the secret room. Inside, Borno greeted me but sniffed me all over, obviously agitated by the signs of my distress. I burst into tears and held him, rocking back and forth and letting my tears fall to his shiny coat.

I regained control over myself and sat up, sniffling. Borno whined and licked my hands.

My body still shook. I needed action. Maybe I would be able to find something else about my father in his office, something we had overlooked last time. In theory no one had been in there. The other scientists had their own labs, and whoever was searching for something had already ransacked the place. So I patted my leg for Borno to follow me and went upstairs.

Once there, the hope and need for action deserted me. I was exhausted. It hit me like a brick wall. I sat down on a chair and fiddled with one of the tablets. Scrolling through the different folder systems, I found one buried under random names and number schemes. I opened the files inside and found my personal information. This was my file. Hidden in plain sight but too many levels down to be obvious. The extra panels Father had done on my bloodwork and testing were in their own file.

I stood and scrambled around in the desks, looking for a drive I could transfer it too. I didn't want to send it over messages for fear of it being intercepted. My shuffling around worried Borno, and he gave a light yelp.

"It's ok. Hush," I said, still digging through a drawer. I finally found a small drive and plugged it in to transfer, when the lights went out.

I turned to face the door.

The lights flicked on again.

"Hello," Galon said.

I didn't answer. I finished the transfer, closed the file system, and pulled the drive, putting it in my pocket as subtly as possible.

"What are you doing up here? Reminiscing?" Galon slid his hand along the table as he circled closer to me. "Ah, you have his dog. How sweet."

I moved a little to my left to get away from the tablet.

"You were late."

My silence seemed to poke at him, so I let it simmer between us.

"They came to me with this plan. I simply didn't stand in their way. But I do still worry that you're slipping. Are you having seizures outside of the controlled situations?"

He strode over to me. I stumbled over a chair and backward, fighting to stay on my feet. I backed into a corner, and Galon came at me like a giant, staring down at me from on high, implying I was nothing more than a cog in the machine.

He put a hand to my forehead as if a fever would indicate anything, as if I had caught a cold and would infect the rest of the ship just because I was acting strangely.

Borno lunged forward, growling. He knew better than to bite, but he put his body between us.

Galon wasn't taking into account that my father had recently disappeared. That I was the best trained and most promising subject the study had ever had. That he was an incompetent ass and couldn't see beyond his flexed biceps.

I wasn't a cocky person, but when it came to Galon, I had absolutely no fear. He had no control over me.

I took hold of Borno's collar and moved to walk past Galon, and he shoved me up against the wall, his arm over my neck, pinning me, not caring that I was all that was holding Borno back.

"I don't think you understand the situation, Selah. This is not some easy test you have to pass. This is not more training. This is real life. Your father is a danger to the system. The WHO wants you to understand that. He has been taken into custody because he presents an idea that could bring down the delicate balance we have, and he could potentially kill the rest of the human race."

That was news to me. I struggled for breath and to keep conscious. Black swam at the edges of my vision, but beyond that I also strained to memorize every word he was saying to me. My fingers clawed at his tensed forearm.

Oxygen flooded my lungs. I fell forward, catching myself on Borno. I wheezed and hacked and sucked in air that burned. My vision flashed brilliant colors.

"Remove the dog," a woman's voice said. A large black blob approached me, and as my vision cleared I could see it was

Darm, or maybe Trej. I didn't have time to react, and he tore Borno from my hands, leaving nothing but the collar.

"Galon, this is not the way," Argana said. She put her hand on his shoulder. A glance passed between them that seemed to hold decades of meaning. I looked back down at the floor to focus on regaining my bodily functions.

"This is your warning to lay off. Leave your father where he is, and we'll leave your mother alone as well," Galon hissed in my ear. He was crouching by me, the room otherwise empty.

And there it came. The blow that I couldn't withstand. I sank into misery. Galon did have control over me because he worked for the people who puppeteered my life. I couldn't risk bringing my mother into all of this, but how could I let it drop that my father had possibly found something big enough to break the strings?

Galon left too.

That was when I felt it. A tiny edge of paper. Tucked into the seams of the collar. Peeking out just enough so someone would find it but not enough that it could be seen. A note.

I tugged it out and opened it flat on the floor.

$$\int_0^\pi \frac{84}{\pi} \cos^2(x)\,dx$$

n bgmp o gvvpxp. cex mdoy nbje pwwez wkks kac svt.
24536 88262 97944

My father's cipher.
I could read half of it.
I know a secret. One that will bring down the WHO.
But the series of numbers I couldn't decipher. He could have been using a different cipher or used the same key but

with numbers. I would have to go find more paper and work it out by hand. Of course the part I could read was nothing new after what Galon had told me, but it was enough to spur me on.

It didn't matter what they threatened. My mother would have said the same. If this secret could break our world, and my father wanted to understand it, then it was necessary to find out what the secret was and bring it to light. It was time I did something.

I would find my father. I would uncover this secret. And I would bring the system to its knees.

CHAPTER NINE

I walked along the scientist's floor in search of Reegan. I strode with purpose, keeping my footsteps quiet but my gait and posture strong. On the inside I was shaking. What kind of eyes did they have on me?

Reegan was a few labs down, in a meeting with the other scientists. Their dogs lay at their feet, and someone was giving a presentation on the wallscreen. Their backs were to me, and I became engrossed in the presentation—a review of every step of the modified project from the macro level. Things certainly didn't look good. It seemed the WHO was either feeding the UN good news or the UN was feeding the people good news. Maybe both. The modified project had flat-lined a while back with a few blips here and there posing as major breakthroughs that never culminated in anything.

I stopped reading the charts to find everyone looking at me.

Reegan said something and got up from his chair. I ducked back away from the window to wait for him.

"What are you doing here?" he hissed once the door was closed. He peeked around behind him to make sure they were back to the presentation.

"We have a problem," I said.

I took him to my father's lab and closed the door, leaning my forehead against it.

"Galon found me here digging through stuff."

Reegan slammed his hand on a table.

"He threatened me," I continued and turned around, "and told me that my father uncovered a secret that could bring down the system. He said they would take my mother if I didn't back off."

Reegan immediately softened. The anger dripped out of him like a squeezed sponge.

"Then we'll leave it alone," he said, so softly I barely heard.

"What? No. My mother, of all people, would slap you for saying that."

The shock on his face was nearly enough to make me laugh, but I didn't.

"If my father found something that big, and I have confirmation that he did, then we need to find it as well and get it out of here. Then we need to find him."

"Ok." Reegan fell into a chair. He combed through his mop of dark brown hair. It would have been sexy if I wasn't coming down from two intense adrenaline rushes and feeling the shakes coming on. "What confirmation do you have?"

"This note. Maybe you can read the rest? I can't get the last line."

He nearly tore it from me. His eyes skimmed the lines and then drifted up to meet mine.

"You can't read the last part. Are you sure? Did you hit your head?"

"You can read it?" I came around to his side to look at it again.

"No. I'm just worried about you."

"Oh." A dead end. I had so hoped it would be as easy as Reegan decoding it, and then we would be done. I had had more than enough stress. I wanted my bed. "Do you have somewhere we can work on this without being seen? My secret room has too many cameras to have easy access at all times."

"Actually, I made some new friends."

"Should we bring other people in on this?"

"No, not like that. They're just helping me understand the ship more, and they have a place we can hide things. But I'll have a key to the room and no one else."

"Are you sure?"

"Very. It's the maintenance crew. In particular a guy named Jimman. He heads up the team down there."

People who had no stake in any of this. People who spent their lives working, eating, and sleeping. But people who might be willing to help us if they understood that we were doing this for the greater good.

"I think we might need them on our side in the future," Reegan said. "It's a good alliance, and they don't even realize we're at war already."

"Now you sound like a UN agent. Can we not make everything about killing people?"

"War isn't about killing people, Selah. War is about power. And all the more power if we can do it without any casualties. So let's make that a priority, ok?" His hand came down on mine, resting on the table next to him. I wanted so badly to yank my hand away, but also to flip it over and grasp his. The confusion tore my heart to shreds.

"Look, I really need some sleep. Can you show me tomorrow and I'll work on this cipher then?"

"Definitely. Go get some rest. You look like you've been through hell today."

His hand squeezed mine. I waited the appropriate amount of time to not be rude and then snatched it away.

"Thanks," I called as I walked out the door.

Reegan convinced me to check the ship again, to see if we could find Father simply by wandering into a room that I knew wasn't accessible by any means I could conceive of and didn't exist on anything except for the original blueprints. I had physically been over the ship a few years ago, and after walking every hallway, testing myself to see if I could avoid the cameras and getting in trouble, I had also checked the building archives and any available information during one winter. So when Reegan proposed we walk the lower levels the next evening, I indulged him. It would be a foray into nostalgia for me.

I continued to ignore the fact that I felt powerless when it came to finding my father. I knew he was on the ship, but I couldn't just meander about without Argana finding out. And even if I could find where he was, would I be able to get us to safety? What did safety even mean at this point? So instead of ripping the place to pieces in a desperate search, I had focused my energy on not acknowledging the pain.

I met Reegan on the fifth floor, and we took the stairs together.

"You know this is unlikely to present anything, right?" I hopped from step to step like a little kid. Having Reegan by my side might make it ok to be seen on the cameras. But there was no guarantee we wouldn't get chastised. This would have to be a quick trip.

"You never know. Maybe I'll see something you didn't see, or maybe you'll see something you didn't see last time. It's a good idea."

I shrugged. "I've got time to waste."

"Is that really how you feel?"

I bit my tongue. My brain told me this was stressful, that I missed my father, that this was the best plan of action for now. My mouth kept producing words that didn't have anything to do with how I actually felt. I missed my father desperately.

"I just don't see how this is going to get us anywhere."

"You're such a surly teenager." He smirked and shoved me. I tripped down a few stairs to the maintenance level. My skin flushed hot, and I turned my face to the floor and went through the doorway.

The hidden rooms were behind the engines, on the far side from where we now stood, so we went into the engine room where the hallway became more of a rickety bridge. It was a walkway attached to the wall, but barely large enough for one person, hanging over the moving parts below. The floor was slatted like the staircases, so it caused even more vertigo. Why they ever thought that was a good idea was beyond me. What if the maintenance workers had a fear of heights?

I looked back at Reegan. He was plastered against the wall, shaking.

"The rooms are over there." I pointed across the vast expanse filled with engines. It was hot and loud, so I had to yell.

Reegan shook his head.

I leaned in closer and yelled again, "The rooms are over there."

He clapped a hand to his ear. "I heard you! I can't move."

"Let's go back in the hallway. This won't get us there anyway."

He jumped from where he was onto the solid metal floor of the hallway. Then he slid to the ground and put his head between his knees. He mumbled something.

I bent down. "What?"

He lifted his head and smacked into my chin. "Ouch!"

"No kidding." I checked my lip for blood. I had bit my tongue.

"I said, the room we can use is through there."

"That might not be the best option if you're freaking out."

"You don't have irrational fears? Then you won't get it. Just give me a minute."

I left him to breathe and studied the machinery pumping in and out, up and down, around and through. I was starting to get impatient when Reegan spoke right by my ear.

"Do you think there's a way to get closer to the hidden rooms?"

I jumped and then collected myself.

"I know there are no bridges across the engines. I think if I remember right we can follow this hallway, and it ends up bisecting a hallway in front of them. But there's no connection between the two. No doorway."

"Let's go take a look."

It wasn't far, but we were met with pure metal. There weren't even any joists or welds to indicate a previous doorway that might have been sealed. There weren't even any cameras since it was a dead end. Reegan ran his hands around the wall looking for a secret lever.

"I've done that," I said.

"I'm doing it again."

He knocked on the metal, and we waited for a response. Nothing.

Reegan finally gave up after another fifteen minutes of going over the wall inch by inch. But as we climbed the stairs, he stopped. "What about the blueprints?"

"They show the rooms, but they don't show any access. Come on, I want a snack." I kept climbing. Yet again my mouth betrayed me. I wasn't hungry; I wanted distraction. Distraction from this horrible helplessness. Argana could take away my father, and she could paralyze me. What hope did I have even if I did manage to find him?

"I want to look at them tonight."

"Ok, whatever." I left him behind knowing I would regret acting so nonchalantly. But for now, it was all I could muster. I wanted to find my father, but this wasn't the way. He had been taken and hidden. He hadn't been placed in a well-known prison where I could visit and speak to him on the other side of a glass wall. It was going to be more difficult than Reegan thought. And I wasn't ready to accept any of it.

Leaving class the next day, Reyla knocked past me in her rush to catch up with the others. I left Henrune and Mag in the lab, discussing some game strategy they were creating for their own simulation. I waved, but they didn't see me.

In the hallway, the others flirted and goofed off. They orbited Kellan like a planet and its moons. Geric stood to the side like his own planet, though he leaned in and laughed whenever they did. Larn glanced back at me and whispered something. The girls giggled. Kellan just smirked.

I took the first turn off the hallway that I could and went

downstairs to my secret room. But as soon as I opened the door, slipped inside, and leaned against the closed door, I couldn't think of why I had come here. There would be no new notes.

Except...

I reached into one of the cubbies and pulled out my uncle's device. I pressed the power button and waited for it to boot. There were no new messages. My hand dropped like it was weighted, and I slid to the floor. I had my forehead on my knees and my eyes closed when I heard a tiny chirp, and a green light blinked on the device. I woke the screen and saw a number two next to the messages app.

I touched it.

I call him Rusty. Isn't he cute? He's a bit antique, hence the nickname. - T

It had worked. Somehow, it had worked. I couldn't imagine what feats of engineering he had needed to accomplish this, but he was talking to me outside of the UN network.

I opened the second message.

Who wrote the autobiography titled Artificial Intelligence?

One of his jokes. A chuckle escaped me. I thought for a moment and sent my answer.

Anne Droid.

I hit send and turned it off again. Then I left the room and headed for the showers in a better mood.

CHAPTER TEN

The next evening after dinner I sat in a dingy, hot room on the lowest level of the ship. It hummed with the sounds of engines and scraping sand and men at work. The noise should have been comforting in its overwhelming intensity, but it worried me that I couldn't hear anyone coming outside the door. I sat at a table, attempting to work out my father's code while Reegan leaned on the table and ate something he had grabbed when he came to get me from the cafeteria.

"What were you looking for in your father's office yesterday?" he asked through a mouthful.

"Anything."

"And what did you find?"

"My file." I didn't know if it was the heat or the noise or the pounding headache that was creeping up on me, but I just didn't want to relay any information. I should have told Reegan about the non-seizure long ago. I should have told him about the extra panels my father had run. But I just didn't feel like it now.

"Interesting. Anything else?"

"Do we have to talk right now?" I snapped.

He held his hands before his face. "Ok."

"Sorry. I don't like this room very much."

"I think it's cozy," Reegan said.

"That's nice for you." I rubbed my temples and took a deep breath. "Is there any water down here?"

Reegan produced a full bottle from behind his back.

"Do you need some alone time?" he teased. I smacked him and then spit water through my teeth at him.

We sat in silence, or without speaking but surrounded by the din, for what seemed like ages while I debated with myself. It was going to come out at some point. It could be the key. I had to tell him.

"There's something I should have told you before."

"This is juicy."

"Seriously. Stop." I set the bottle on the table and took a deep, steadying breath. "When we entered the ship on the first day of summer and we all went into a controlled seizure... I didn't seize."

Reegan's face said it all. I was going to die. I should say my farewells now while I still had the chance.

"Does your father know?"

"Thank you for speaking in present tense about him. Let's keep that up. I like it."

"Stop avoiding, Selah." He crouched down in front of me. "Does he know? Did he figure out why?"

"He was the only one who saw when it happened. I pretended after I saw the look on his face. It terrified me, just like your face right now."

"Oh come on, I'm not that ugly." The joke fell flat.

"He wasn't able to fully figure it out, or if he did, he didn't tell me."

"The extra panels on you."

"You noticed?"

"He hid them behind his back. I made note of that. It was odd. He hadn't hidden anything from me before."

"I found the results when I found my file."

Reegan's face lit up. He held his hand out, and I placed my tablet in it, unlocked and opened to the folder I had transferred.

"My entire life is on there. Please don't get personal about it. Ok?" I tried to lighten the mood again, but I could have cut the air with a knife. Between the heat and the stress, we were both on the edge of a precipice. One that stood before an unknown abyss. Who knew what had changed in my body to make the seizures not work anymore?

"I watched the broadcast that we did just before your father disappeared. This is why he said it was weird I hadn't outgrown the seizures. He thought you had outgrown them. But if he already had the panels, then why hypothesize that? He had to have known that wasn't the case."

"Maybe he hadn't figured it out yet. Maybe he figured it out after your seizure but before they took him, based on what he learned from you."

All this time Reegan's eyes danced over the information on the tablet. I left him to it and tried to focus on the code again, but I kept reading the same equation over and over, my brain unable to comprehend.

"You're healthy as a human before The Thinning," Reegan said. "According to these at least. But these don't get into your DNA strands and the genetic code that causes our seizures. That code was implemented after the first batch of modified proved to be worse off than normal humans. They were sickly and unable to control their body temperature to a degree that without a perfect environment—some sort of controlled box they could never leave—the babies would just seize to death. The seizures were implemented as a control to make sure we were seizing from the science, not from the other factors like neural tube defects and reduced sweat glands. You know, the type of stuff our parents suffer from. Anyways, I would have to get that information to make sure you aren't sick like the first modified."

The words were out there. He had said it. I was probably, most likely, presumably sick.

One arm thumped onto the table before me like dead weight. My head followed to rest on it. Reegan caressed my back, and I turned to face him. He folded me into his body, protective and soothing. Tears didn't come, but neither did a panic attack. I was in shock.

In an attempt to ignore the stress of possibly being on my way to my deathbed, I trained harder and added in coding work every evening. I was getting nowhere with my father's note, but working with the numbers soothed my brain into a stupor so I didn't have to spend any waking moments thinking about my fate. Trudging to and from the maintenance level only added to my conditioning, so my body felt more in shape than ever. And the weekly tests that Reegan and the other scientists ran on my group were showing it. I was surpassing the group in toning.

One night I went down the stairs and didn't really check

behind me before I entered the room. I set my things next to the table when the door opened again behind me. I whipped around, my heart pounding, really hoping it was Reegan.

It wasn't.

"I wondered where you were hiding." Galon stepped inside and shut the door behind him, sitting in a chair that blocked me in.

"What do you want?" My voice shook against my wishes.

"I'm here to ask why you haven't found your father yet? Though you seemed capable of incredible hatred only two years ago. I suppose it makes sense." He studied his fingernails.

But today, in this cramped and hot room, I worried Galon had more in mind than just words.

"Don't bother tensing your muscles," Galon said. "I'm not going to do anything. I just want you to understand what should really happen in this world. What happened to my dog, my sweet Jayd, is what should happen to all of us. We should burn in the fires of hell for what we've done. This world is meant to end with us. We aren't destined to begin evolving again."

He left the room so abruptly, I barely realized he was gone until the door clicked shut. The hum of the engines filled my ears, alongside the rush of blood pumping through my veins.

***

The holo-studio seemed my only solace now.

I ended up in the holo-studio, attempting to force my stress away through repetitive motion and sweat. Usually I could get into a rhythm that would shut down my brain, but this time it just wasn't working. As I went from one stance to the next, my brain hopped from fear of Galon, to terror over an unknown disease invading my bloodstream, to flutters related to my ever-increasing crush on Reegan, to extreme need to touch my father again.

I gave up and went to the comms room to see if my mother could blow the blues from my thoughts.

Her message wasn't exactly uplifting, but the sight of her face, though I couldn't touch it, was comforting at least. She sat in her armchair, absently stroking Bearna, telling me what was happening in the cities.

She made sure to walk the ramparts every day when it was cool enough, so she could see the borders herself. She ingratiated herself in the market and community so she had an ear to the ground. This was nothing new. If my father was a scientist, my mother was an anthropologist. She knew people.

"Everyone seems rather upbeat about the new developments coming from the ship. I know that the morale of the people is important. Obviously the UN knows that as well. So keep your chin up, Selah. Mindset has great control over stress levels and ability to function. I'm sure even your father would say that..." She trailed off at the mention of my father.

"Anyways," she continued, "We're just fine here. Please let me know how you're doing and if you've heard anything."

The hologram melted away.

I stood to record an answer.

Yet again I was conflicted. I couldn't tell her about our plans to find Father. If the WHO was listening to messages, I would be destroyed. I couldn't tell her of my fear of Galon—there was nothing she could do, and it would only worry her. I knew nothing more about Father, so there was no reason to mention it. I made my decision and signaled for recording.

"I have a boy problem, Mother. I would love your insight. See, I have a crush. On a boy. I said that already. Ok, here goes. I think I'm falling for Reegan."

I stopped.

I signaled to erase the entire recording. Signaled again to begin.

"I have a friend who has a problem, and I wondered if you might have something to say about it. She's falling for someone, but she's not sure he's the right person for her, or that anyone is right for her at all. She's a bit of a loner, besides me of course, because I'm her friend, and that's why I'm looking to help her with this issue and... Oh, screw it."

I waved to erase again, took a deep breath, and started recording.

"I miss you, Mother."

Then I signaled the system to send it.

I left the room, hoping to find relief in sleep at least.

CHAPTER ELEVEN

"Selah!" Reegan burst into the holo-studio early one morning. My heart jumped up to choke me.

"What the hell? Why did you have to freak me out like that?"

"Sorry." He took in the empty studio with the lights low. "I miss being in here. I miss the smell, the feel of the floor." He bounced on his toes. "But why are you working without a holo?"

"I prefer it." I left it at that. "What do you want?"

"I found another note hidden within your panel results. I can read it. It's a coordinate type system pointing somewhere on the ship. I think your father hid something for us to find."

"It's like a scavenger hunt. Why couldn't he have just told us? This is getting ridiculous."

"What if this is the last thing?"

I threw my hands in the air. "We know it's not the last thing. I still have half a message to decode from the note on Borno's collar. How did my father have the time to devise this elaborate hide and seek but not have time to just come find me and tell me?"

"Maybe he was creating this all along as a safety net." Reegan put his hands behind his back and scrubbed one foot on the floor. If I didn't know better, I'd have said he looked sheepish. Maybe the little boy inside was peeking through the cocky man. It was endearing, and I wanted to give him a peck on the cheek.

"You like this." I came up and circled him. "You enjoy this game of chess. You want to see who wins. But the question is, do you care who the winner is as long as the game is interesting?" I poked him in the chest.

His head snapped up. "How could you say that to me?"

"Well?"

"Did you know that I don't have parents anymore?"

"I'm sorry." I stopped moving. Yet again my mouth was saying things my heart didn't mean.

"I love your father very much." He poked me back. "I'm invested in finding him, not in playing some game. Now if we're on the same page, I'd like your help locating whatever he's hidden at these coordinates." He swiveled and left the room.

I stood in shock for a moment, then ran after him. "I have training."

"We'll find it before you have to be there. You've got plenty of time."

"No really, I can't afford to be late again. Galon will kill me."

"Galon can stuff it. I'll talk to him if I need to."

I tugged on Reegan's shirt to stop him. "Please don't do that. I've had enough teasing for a lifetime. I don't need a knight in shining armor."

Something flickered across Reegan's face. It was like a flash of a memory or dream, not easy to interpret, but evocative and powerful. He nodded and turned to keep walking. We went up to level six, where my generation lived, and around a few corners until we were directly above my secret room.

"What are we doing here? There's no room here. I've looked."

"This is where the coordinates lead. So there has to be something here. Look around. Maybe the lever you push has a twin up here?"

I felt around, over, and under metal beams. We tapped on the walls and stepped lightly on the floor while listening for differences.

As we continued our search, the clipping of heels on metal sounded down the hallway. We looked at each other, stopped what we were doing, and pretended to be leaning against the wall in conversation.

Argana came around the corner. She slowed when she saw us, then she stopped in front of us. "How are you two today?" she asked, her voice cheery. A few new wrinkles showed around her lips and forehead. All the stress of a failing project was getting to her. The bags under her eyes only added to the effect.

"Doing well," Reegan answered. He was so diplomatic. Capable of answering just as brightly and quickly reacting to anything. "How about you?"

"I'm good. What are you up to? It looks like a strange mating dance on the cameras. Shouldn't Selah be in training?" Her hands went to her hips. She huffed a little bit, like a frustrated toddler not getting her way.

I had no response. I wanted to say fourteen different things, all of them rude, but none of them would order themselves properly in my brain to make their way to my mouth and out. The highest priority would have been to show her that she shouldn't speak about someone in third person when they're standing in front of you. Reegan spoke before I could get control of myself.

"You're headed there now, aren't you?" He addressed me. "We were discussing some of her results from the testing. We thought there was something a little bit off, but it turns out she hadn't been feeling well that day, so it was just a little cold. It's a good explanation for the results we saw. And as for the dance, we were practicing for a small concert the first generation is putting on for the scientists. I asked Selah to help me with my part."

Argana stared at him, one eyebrow raised. After too much silence, she finally said, "Ok. I want to make sure the subjects stay healthy and on top of their game. Let's make sure that's the case."

Reegan nodded.

The next moment dragged into the future endlessly. I feared she wouldn't leave, and I would have to go to training without finding the secret my father had hidden here. But after an eternity, she continued on her way with clippier clops and her arms rigid by her sides.

Reegan shrugged his shoulders.

When she was definitely gone, I scaled the wall and looked around the ceiling. It seemed there was nothing, and time was running short before I needed to be in training. Then I saw it. A tiny button in the crevice between wall and ceiling where the door to my secret room would have been. When I reached up and pushed it, a small door popped open near the floor. I dropped down nearly on top of Reegan when he dashed forward to get to the opening.

He reached in and produced a journal. A real, paper journal.

It was then that I looked at the time and took off running. The journal would have to wait.

After an incredibly tiring day, I looked at the stairs leading to the lower levels and groaned. My knees and calves would not thank me in the morning. I took that first step anyway and soon found myself at the bottom in front of the door to our lair. Someone behind me cleared their throat as I lifted my hand to knock. I spun around.

"Oh, hello Jimman." It was the head of maintenance, a man Reegan had introduced me to when we acquired the key.

"Everything all right? You look tired."

"I'm fine. Was there something you needed?"

"Well, the guys just wanted to check. You've been down here a lot, is there a problem?"

"Problem? Problem with…"

"We don't care what you're hiding. Reegan explained vaguely what might be happening, and that you are Dr. Beechwood's daughter. We just want to know if there's anything we can do. We work for the UN, not the WHO. And we have respect for your father. I'm sorry that he's gone missing. Is that why you're down here so much?"

I felt another string in my inner stress ball snap and wither. I couldn't help but smile.

"Yes." The honesty felt good, really good. "We're trying to find him. Do you know anything?"

Jimman rocked on his feet. "Sorry, I don't. But I know this ship like the back of my hand, if you ever need anything in that topic, I'm your man."

I smiled.

Jimman nodded and continued on down the walkway that stood over the engines. I waited for a moment and then faced the door.

I tapped gently.

"Selah?" Reegan said from the other side.

I pushed the door open.

"Glad it's you."

"Do you have the journal? What does it say?"

"A lot. Come look."

He flipped pages back to one about a third of the way in.

Selah is changing. Of course that's expected as she's going through puberty. But I'm noticing changes I wasn't quite expecting. Her skin and hair are darkening at a rapid pace. She has this beautiful speck in her eye that is almost a navy color. I'll have to keep track of any major changes over the winter in case they become significant.

I turned the pages as I read. The feel of the paper was soft and flimsy, different than the metal of the ship or the plastic of our training weapons or the glass of my tablet. Father noted my growth and anything interesting. Most of it seemed natural, nothing out of the ordinary. He even noted through the summer how I was excelling at my training. Though he also noted how I wasn't surpassing expectations, only that I was top of my generation. He made a note that it might be due to my personality, to the fact that I was incredibly determined.

Reegan laughed when we read that one. Each entry was dated. And soon we got to the beginning of this summer.

Selah did something today that shouldn't have happened. This one specific thing worries me as it's not something a healthy modified should do. It's very possible there's something wrong either with her gene mutation or with her entire system.

I felt comforted by his words and also repelled, seeing as he confirmed my worst fears. I was no child of his. He spoke of me like I was a robot. I was an experiment and something of interest to him. But that was all.

This is reminiscent of the first generation. That's why it terrifies me.

He skirted the actual topic, never mentioned what had really happened, probably to protect the secret if anyone found this journal. If I was sick, the entire ship and the entire project were in danger. He had obviously thought of that right away. I could bring down the human race if I brought the SE bacteria to this oasis in the desert.

The next date said only this: *Something is different about Selah, but I now know she isn't sick.*

I lifted my head to find Reegan staring at me. He reached across the table to wipe my cheek, and his finger came away wet. He stepped around the table and pulled me into a hug. It was reassuring to have my father's statement, but there was still this huge unknown circling me like a vulture. If I wasn't sick, then why hadn't I seized? What was wrong with me?

I leaned back enough to look Reegan in the eye. He brushed my hair away from my face and then cupped my cheek. Blood rushed to the surface of my skin, and my entire body heated. He bent down and put his lips to mine. It was soft and wet and squishy and weird. Flat out weird. Like kissing a pillow. The blood that had risen immediately cooled, and I jerked away.

We looked at each other and then burst out laughing.

I wiped my mouth.

"I had wondered, but now I know," Reegan said with a chuckle.

"Know what?" I didn't want to be the one to admit it. If I

was wrong, I would hurt his feelings. But that had been like kissing a best friend, a brother. It was so wrong. My crush dissipated immediately into bright friendship.

"We're meant to just be friends?" He held out a hand for me to take. We shook and then laughed some more.

A loud bang outside the door stopped us. We paused to listen, but there was nothing more.

"Let's go," Reegan said. "You need a shower at least." His wrinkled nose and wicked grin sent me into another fit of hysteria.

He closed the journal and tucked it into a pocket in his coat. He took me to level six and then wished me goodnight as he climbed higher.

I turned back and went to floor five. I wanted to see if my uncle had left another joke. It would be the highlight on a good day.

There was a message, and it was a joke. A good one.

Clever you. How about this one? Why did the robot go back to school? - T

It took me a moment, and then a grin burst onto my face. It was so stupid and so funny.

He was getting a bit rusty.

I left the secret room and swung my arms as I walked, feeling lighter after the release of at least a few of my stresses. But at the entrance to the showers, Galon blew by me to get out. He turned back as he walked away and barked at me like a dog. I shivered and fell back into my nest of panic. Even a shower wasn't going to wash away that feeling.

CHAPTER TWELVE

"Wake!" a voice belted into the room.

I opened my eyes and noticed some of the others moving around and grumbling.

"All generations will be in the holo-studio together today. Then tomorrow the science team will run extensive tests on your systems. Today you will work in conjunction with the other generations to complete a more difficult simulation." The WHO guard who had come in to inform us, marched back out.

"Awesome," Kellan said. "Now I can get five more minutes." He rolled over.

No one touched him, though he should have been kicked. If he was late, we were all in trouble.

I threw the covers back and forced myself awake with a vigorous rub of my face. I was washed and dressed within minutes, working on pinning my long hair into a braid and away from my face when Kellan finally rolled from his bunk. Most everyone else had left except for a few who were closest to him. I left too, planning on skipping breakfast but at least getting something to drink.

I was sipping my bottle of water as I walked when Kellan barreled past me in the hall.

"Hurry up, Selah. You'll get us in trouble." He cackled.

I walked into a holo-studio filled to the brim with people. How they planned on using all of us during a skirmish I had no idea. But then I noticed the mats and the tablets stacked in a corner. This would be a mental exercise. Strange when we would have check-ups tomorrow. Were they going to run brain scans?

People milled about, the youngest generation goofing off as usual. Kellan seemed to feed off the energy. He was bouncing off the walls. He did a few laps around the room, dodging people, and ran smack into me so that we both ended up sprawled on the floor.

"Sorry." He grinned down at me but made no move to get off.

I stayed stock still. I didn't want him to have any reason to say something crude.

"I'll just be going." He hopped up and took off running again.

A hand appeared over my face, and I grabbed it. When I was halfway to standing, I let go as I finally saw Galon. I fell straight back onto the floor with a thud.

Galon chuckled and offered his hand again. I used my own power to stand.

"Attention!" a voice by the door screamed. "Formation please, by age, youngest at the front right corner. My right."

There was no scrambling, no confusion. We knew our ages. We knew our order. We knew our positions. Within minutes the formation was set in parallel lines with extreme precision. The youngest child was at the front right, the oldest at the rear left. I looked around me without moving my head and took in the variety of modified children. We all had similar traits—darker skin, darker eyes and hair, tall and lean, fit—but besides those few things, we were as varied as grains of sand.

While our genes had been significantly modified, they also came originally from our respective parents. We didn't match them exactly as they had all grown pale due to the environment, no matter their ancestry. So we all exhibited features according to the generations of normal humans who came before us. But as I looked at the gradient of skin colors around me, I noticed I was rather dark. I was even darker than the younger generation, who had been enhanced further than my own. I knew my eyes were dark, but my hair was also a darker shade, almost black instead of one of their varying shades of brown. In all this desert of sand, I felt like the odd one out. Of course I had commonly felt like that since I rarely got along with my generation, but now I noticed the differences my father had noted in his journal.

After inspection and some deliberating between the leaders, Argana stepped up to speak. As always, she looked tiny standing between two large men, their arms crossed. Was she ever without them?

"You will work as one team. Your first task is to select three leaders by popular vote. These leaders need to exhibit skills that include strategy but also cunning and confidence. You might be swayed to choose from the oldest generation, but we would advise that you at least hear out candidates from the other generations as you all have different skill sets due to different styles of training. After you've selected leaders, those people will delegate tasks to everyone else, including that of navigation, weaponry, defense, and systems maintenance. You will be handed tablets fit for your purpose in the skirmish. The leaders have the ability to switch the tablets around as the simulation progresses in case they haven't placed people correctly. But they are only allowed three switches each."

"It's a giant game of chess with the queens chosen by democracy," someone behind and to my left whispered.

"The simulation will last as long as it takes you to defeat your common enemy," Argana continued. "Please begin."

The room probably should have burst into chaos, with everyone who desired leadership raising their voices to be heard. But we were a well-trained group, and we settled into our particular generations to choose leaders who would then be put before the entire assembly as candidates. It was all orderly and controlled. An outsider might have even said eerie since it was a room full of children locked in organized whispers.

Each generation sent two candidates forward. Ours included Kellan and Geric. They each presented their cases for leadership. I breathed a sigh of relief when Kellan was not chosen. It was all done within a half hour. Argana conferred with the leaders and supposedly explained the situation. The herd was kept in the dark.

Then our leaders passed out tablets and mats. We ordered ourselves according to the color of our tablets—the navigators sitting with navigators, the gunmen with gunmen, the defense team together in a circle, and the miscellaneous crew scattered around.

The leaders wandered among us as the simulation began, the eldest with her hands behind her back like a professor, the youngest marching to and fro without really caring whose fingers he mashed, and Geric pausing to check that everyone was comfortable and settled.

The metal panel closed slowly over the solarglass as our world became a universe speckled with stars and planets and asteroids. A few oohs and aahs spread around the room. Forty spaceships jumped into view. Our tablets sprang to life with controls and information. This was an enemy fleet. They had come to destroy the planet. Secretly I loved that we were escaping our own mess of a planet to defend it. It seemed ironic. For once I didn't have to dodge leaves.

The leaders did their work—positioned us all properly to defeat the fleet with our scant force. But as time went on, it was obvious we were losing ground. They conferred and made a few switches. I did my work as a gunner, but my brain couldn't stop wandering. I wanted to understand the purpose. Why were they pushing us through something that had nothing to do with our current situation? They had never presented simulations that took us off world. They had never asked us to defeat anything other than our own plant and animal life. This was a tactical practice and required a lot of coordination. But why?

Geric tapped me on the shoulder to exchange places with a navigation crew member. As soon as I had the new tablet with code streaming past, I was able to correct a bug in the system and gain control of half of our ships that had wandered off course. The weaponry had made no sense to me, and I hadn't been properly assigned. But now, with my skills in their rightful place, the chess board could be taken. The enemy battleships began falling to our gunmen. This had been a tactical test. One intended to play to our strengths without using any physical force. And then I knew.

The testing tomorrow would center around our brain function. They would probably run simple knowledge tests to see how our brains lit up in MRI. They were grasping for straws. Our bodies weren't evolving. They wanted to see if our brains might be.

The realization made sitting in an isolation tank the next day all the more excruciating. Knowing their purpose made it feel as if the readings would be askew and useless. So instead of paying attention to their inane *what is two plus two* and *what shape is this* questions, I sifted through the words from my father's journal that I could remember.

I also recalled the code I had found on Borno's collar. I had spent weeks working through possibilities for solving it, so the numbers were burned in my memory with perfect clarity. It was a mathematical equation that made absolutely no sense. Typically Father's codes actually worked as math. It was the best way to hide something, by making it look like something else. The perfect camouflage. But the second half of his note that I still couldn't decipher made no sense whatsoever. It didn't equal four, like two plus two did.

The scientists wandered around us with their noses glued to their tablets. A time or two one of them tripped over a cord running on the floor or the edge of a tank.

As I thought about the code, I recalled the spacing of the numbers had been wonky. As if he had grouped certain numbers together. It was also super simplified. There was no calculus or trigonometry. I shook my head to try to forget about it for the time being, and my sensors went nuts. A scientist stepped up to check the machines and feel around my head. He never looked me in the eye or spoke to me, just poked and prodded me and then touched some selections on the tablet in front of my face that was giving me commands. I had never felt more like a science experiment than at that moment—locked in a gel tank, unable to move, and being ignored like the lab rat I apparently was to this man.

Compare these patterns and find the common shape.

"A square," I said.

"No need to answer aloud. We're monitoring your brain waves not your speech." The scientist still didn't look at me. When he walked away, I wanted to scream the words at his back. *A square!*

If 4/24/1998 is a date, then which number denotes the month in 5/6/1998.

"Five," I said.

And suddenly it all made sense.

My father's code.

The journal.

The groupings of numbers.

They corresponded.

My body went into motion. I started wriggling and fussing, attempting to break free from an iron prison built for my body shape. The gel moved slightly as I thrashed, but the metal casing went nowhere. My sensors buzzed and dinged and made a huge ruckus. A few scientists came running over.

"Is she seizing?" one said.

"I'm not seizing!" I screamed. "Let me out!"

Reegan came up behind the group and stood there grinning like an ape.

"Reegan. Stop staring at me and open this thing!"

He crossed his arms.

"Can I have a reason why? You're in the middle of the test."

"I figured something out. I need to go test my theory."

"Are you a scientist now?" one of the scientists said. "Be still, child. You'll hurt yourself. You'll be out of there when the test is finished." He huffed and turned to go back to his work. The others left as well. Reegan stayed, chuckling under his breath.

"Let me out," I growled.

"I can't, Selah. Have patience, ok?"

"How fast do these questions go?" I watched the screen and started answering as fast as I could. The tablet flipped through the slides as quickly as I answered. When it was finished, the system rang shrilly, and my isolation tank popped open with a hiss.

I jumped out, glistening with sweat and chilled from the blast of cool air. But at this point, that didn't matter. I threw on the robe Reegan held out for me and ran from the room.

I sprinted all the way down to the maintenance level. I passed Jimman on the way but didn't do more than wave. Stretching my legs felt amazing after two days of stagnating. I turned through a small arch onto the walkway that hung over the engines. The heat of the room hit me and nearly knocked me over. I was already panting and sweating, but this was on a level beyond what my body could handle.

I stepped back around the corner to catch my breath. With that little bit of a pause, I patted my pockets to find the key to the door only to discover I was wearing a robe that had randomly been handed to me.

Luckily, Reegan came walking down the hall with a smug

look I wanted to wipe from his face with a coarse rag. I hugged the robe tighter and stuck my tongue out at him.

"I assumed you were coming down here. I take it as a good sign that you weren't followed. I've got the key, if you were wondering. You left it in your pants up above. Maybe you should consider getting dressed before going for a jog around the ship?"

I punched him in the shoulder and held my hand out for the key, as well as my clothes.

"You seem a little agitated. I think I'll open the door." Reegan laughed and squeezed past me through the archway.

The roar from the engines was significantly louder once through the arch, and the heat blasted me again. This time it didn't feel like a wave of exhaustion, so I let it come and followed Reegan.

Inside the room, I yanked my pants on under the robe before he shut the door. When he did, the temperature plummeted back down, and I felt nearly naked again with just an undershirt on. I pulled my shirt on and then pulled out the journal and the code. I flipped pages until I got to the first one that corresponded with the code.

"Here. Look!" My finger pointed at the string of numbers at the top. They were where someone would write a date, and I had originally thought they *were* dates, but they were much longer than any date. Knowing my father, they were some nerdy reference to star dates or something else.

We read the page together. It wasn't one we had seen before as it came long before the page with my non-seizure.

Vanishing twins.

That was it. Two words on a page. Two tiny words that made absolutely no sense to me whatsoever.

"Do you know what that means?" Reegan asked.

"No idea."

"I think it could refer to when a twin is reabsorbed."

"By the ether?"

"Ha. By the womb. When the cells are just developing, one twin can perish and be reabsorbed. But why would he write that there?"

I flipped to the page before.

Results show that the athyrium filix-femina *plant we were working with was not infected with* Staphylococcus evolutio, *and therefore the research proved pointless. We'll have to wait for another chance to gather other specimens...*

I shuffled the pages by to get to the one after.

The numbers for folate that I've been watching on the current pregnancies are resulting in nothing. The mothers and babies are growing well, but their folate is only being maintained artificially. There are no visible neural tube defects, but the mothers are not creating their own folate based on artificial sunlight treatments...

Nothing. It was in the middle of two totally unrelated topics. Unless one of the mothers he had been monitoring had a vanishing twin?

A knock sounded on the door. I shoved the journal and code in a drawer, and Reegan went to answer it.

It was Jimman.

"I just want to let you know there's someone wandering around down here. Not sure if they're looking for you. I didn't say anything."

"Thanks. We'll head upstairs. Hope you have a good night." Reegan said.

I put the journal and code in my waistband, stood, and followed Reegan out the door. He locked it behind us, and we took the stairs in sync, both lost in our thoughts.

"Come back with me to my room," Reegan said.

I giggled. "What?"

"Sorry. I should have clarified." A grin cracked across his face. "We can do more research in private there."

"Research?" I wiggled my eyebrows.

"Wow Selah. Wow. Is your mind always in the gutter?"

I shoved him so he stumbled and had to grab me for balance. Then I continued beyond level six with him.

Lying on his bunk, bouncing a ball against the ceiling, I felt completely at home. It made me wonder what would happen that winter. Would he spend even more time at our home? Of course if Father never came back...

I let the *pong* of the ball on the metal stop that thought in its tracks.

"That's interesting." Reegan had been muttering things like that for the past hour, crouched over his tablet at the table. His room barely allowed for walking around those two pieces of furniture. But it was comfortable cozy, not ridiculously tight. Even with two people inside. And without the heat and hum of giant engines, it was definitely a step above our other option.

"I'd never thought of that," he said.

"Find anything interesting?" I asked.

"Some things."

The air filled with silence again, so I broke that with another bounce of the ball.

"Do you have to do that?"

"Sorry."

I kept the ball but alternated squeezing it and tossing it to the other hand. Even that made a pretty loud *thwak* in this tiny room. Reegan glared at me.

"Give me something to do if you don't want me to be annoying," I said.

"There *is* nothing to do." He picked his chair up and spun it backwards. Then he plunked down again. "Vanishing twins are what I thought. They're a deceased twin who is reabsorbed in the womb. Granted, if the twin dies after the first trimester, there can be more difficulty. But in the first trimester, the twin is either completely reabsorbed or, after the embryonic stage, the tissues can be flattened to create room for the surviving twin."

"Great. Still doesn't tell us why my father wrote it down." I tossed the ball again.

Reegan caught it before it hit the ceiling. "I have a theory about that."

"One of the mothers he was monitoring had a vanishing twin."

"Yes." Reegan leaned forward.

"And?" I leaned forward as well.

"The only generation that was tested with artificial sunlight for folate was your generation."

I sat up.

"So what if *you* are the surviving twin?"

"Ok. Still doesn't tell us why it's important."

"No, it doesn't." Reegan slumped over his legs.

We had both felt on the cusp of discovery and now plummeted into the despair of a lost trail. Exhaustion hit me, and I realized how late it was.

"I'll get in trouble if I go through the halls this late alone," I said.

"I'll take you back down." He stashed the journal in his desk.

The hallway lights were dimmed. It was later than I had thought. Our footsteps echoed, bouncing around the metal and announcing our presence to anyone and everyone.

We reached my door where I had planned to slide in unnoticed, but Galon stood just inside as if he had been waiting an inch inside the door for the past few hours.

"This is another mark on your record, Selah," he hissed. I stepped aside so he could see Reegan behind me.

"Hello Galon," Reegan said. "Selah required further testing because of her results on the MRI. But I was sure you had been informed of that? No? Now you have been." He pivoted and walked away before Galon could gather his breath for a rebuttal. He snapped his mouth shut and let me into the room.

But then we heard footsteps. We both looked into the corridor and found one of Argana's henchmen stomping our way. Galon crossed his arms and smirked at me.

"I've been sent to check that everything is ok," Trej said. "Selah was seen out of bed. Argana wants to be sure she's not ill or had a mishap."

I didn't dare chuckle. Unfortunately Reegan hadn't seen Trej galumphing his way down the hall from the other direction, so I didn't have my shield in place. I kept a straight face and said, "I'm fine. Just had some more tests to run but everything looks ok. Thanks for being so thoughtful and coming to check on me." Then I pulled a Reegan and about-faced before I could get in further trouble.

CHAPTER THIRTEEN

Today was my birthday. Ironic that we might have found out I had been a twin. Maybe that was why I never fit in. Maybe I belonged with my twin, and she (or he) hadn't survived to be a loner with me. I didn't want to get out of bed, but I couldn't afford to be late, so I flipped the covers off.

Dive into the deep end, Mother always said.

I had thought the room was cold, but when my feet touched the metal floor, it was even more of a shock. I was alone in the room.

I ran to the holo-studio to catch up with the others. I spent the day in silence, answering questions with grunts and nods. I pushed my body hard, and it felt good. My muscles rewarded me with stunning strength, and my ligaments stretched to perfection. I felt on top of the world.

I grabbed lunch and left the cafeteria to check messages. I was good at maneuvering the popular areas of the ship at unpopular times. It was a dance I had practiced for years now. The job of keeping myself alone was full time.

I opened a message from my mother and snacked while I watched.

"Hello my darling girl. Today is your birthday, so I thought I would share a birthday memory from when you used to celebrate at home. This was before you quite realized you were built of a mixture of me, your father, and science. You still thought fairies were real. You loved celebrating your birthday. I'm pretty sure you hit your cynical streak soon after this because when I went back to watch the years after, you weren't quite as bubbly and interested in the festivities." She laughed.

I was glad she could laugh at how pessimistic I was. It meant there was hope for me.

She hit the button on the hologram within her hologram, and we watched it, in a way, together. It was a party of epic proportions. Tiny me walked into a room decorated with my presents—a few paintings created with natural dyes and pots of paint for me to create my own masterpieces, a new dress with a long skirt and in a dark shade of blue, and a photo on my tablet of the three of us standing on top of the rampart with a perspective that made it look like we were in the jungle instead of miles away from it.

"Thank you!" I squeaked. My voice was tinny and annoying.

I hated it. But I remembered the feeling of hugging my father and then my mother. Inhaling their scents, feeling protected, jumping up and down with boundless energy. Mother pulled out the paint and some precious paper, and we got to work on scenes full of fairies and rainbows and green. Green was my absolute favorite color at the time. In fact, it probably still was, though I rarely thought in terms of "favorites" anymore.

Mother stopped the hologram.

She had tears in her eyes.

"I love you."

Her hologram abruptly stopped. It sent a bolt of fear through me, but then I remembered she was going through an incredibly frustrating time. Her beloved soul mate was missing, and there was nothing she could do about it.

I pulled up the messaging system and wrote her a long letter.

Mother,

I'll be polite first and say thank you for the birthday wishes and the beautiful memory. It's certainly not as fun or interesting celebrating my birthday on the ship so far from you. There's nothing I want more today than to be able to hug you. But I appreciate that you find my cynicism funny. You've always accepted me for who I am, even if I'm crotchety and sullen or bubbly and upbeat. That makes you truly the best of mothers. You are capable of loving me while also letting me be.

Of course, with our circumstances you've probably been forced into that more than a mother should be. I wonder if I'll ever be a mother and if I'll be able to keep distance from my child while still smothering them with love? You would probably simply say, "Of course you will." And that, Mother, would be because I've learned from the best.

I still haven't heard about Father. I'm so sorry to have to write that.

Reegan and I have been doing some research into things. We recently found information on vanishing twins. It's an interesting subject. Do you know anything about it? Basically it's when a twin dies in the womb and is reabsorbed by the mother. The surviving twin can still make it through gestation. It makes me think about how many people might be missing their other half when they didn't even know it. If I had had a twin, that birthday and all birthdays would have been much different. Would I have liked sharing a birthday? Or would I have wanted one of my own? Would you have made two dresses? Or a dress and a pair of pants? It brings up so many possibilities when you think how life could have been completely altered by one moment in time—the death of someone you didn't even know existed.

I will sleep with your scarf around my face tonight and dream that I'm lying beside you.

I love you too.

Selah

I sent the message without rereading and logged out. What was done was done. My mother would either know what the heck I was talking about or would assume I was going crazy out here on this floating island in the desert.

I left the comms room and still had time before the next training session. My life was beginning to feel beyond controlled. I had my schedule. I had my requirements. I had my limits. It was all starting to sound like too much, so I took the long way back to the holo-studio. That took me down one hallway after another, each a long tunnel of metal disappearing around corners or into the distance. Tiny and constricting but seemingly endless. It also took me by my secret room. I checked both directions of the hallway and saw no one. I tapped the lever to open the door. A piece of paper fluttered to the ground as I squeezed through. I snatched it from the ground and shut the door softly.

It wasn't Father's handwriting.

But it was easily decoded. Reegan wanted to compare my DNA to the SE bacteria that held us captive. He had a theory. The ship had old logs of SE DNA, but he had already compared them. The bacteria changed so swiftly that he wanted fresh samples. To do that we would have to get to the jungle and out of the ship, then bring it back to the ship to study. He would risk exposing the entire ship. What theory did he have that was worth that? All of these people's lives? The modification project? Most of the brains behind the WHO?

He didn't go into further detail, but my brain took the information and ran with it. He thought I was sick. That had to be it. He had to prove that I had the SE bacteria inside me by comparing the molecular structures. He had seen a foreign body in my bloodstream in the extra panels. What else could it possibly be? I had to be sick. How was I still alive? How had I not infected the ship? Was I a carrier? What if someone touched my blood? Like my father had when the needle drawing my blood had poked through his glove.

I put my forehead against the cool wall to calm the blood rushing through my system. What if my father was dead, and that was the secret? They had pulled him out of the ship because they needed to protect everyone else. My father was dead. He was in the desert somewhere, abandoned, his body being buried by every gust of sand, his bones bleaching in the harsh sun.

My breathing increased. My heart fluttered on every second or third beat. The edges of my vision burned black. I feared a seizure was coming on. I flipped around to lean against the wall and slid down to hug my knees. I slapped my cheek.

The adrenaline coursing through my veins made every part of me tingle. I wanted out, but I didn't dare move. I hungered for sky, for air, for something that wasn't these metal walls closing in on me. When I didn't black out after a few minutes, my mind grasped at straws. Had I been able to somehow fend it off? Was I having a heart attack? Was I having a panic attack?

I clenched my hands and forced myself to breathe slowly and deeply. Then I took the time to relax each and every muscle from my head to my toes. When I had finished that the room wasn't spinning anymore, my heart wasn't leaping anymore.

I pulled old Rusty out, hoping to be calmed even further by my uncle's notes.

Don't believe them, darling girl. They don't know what they think they know.

I slammed a fist against the wall. Why did they all have to be so damn cryptic?

What, no joke? Did you have a bad day?

I wanted to say something nastier, but I didn't have the brain power for it. After sending the message, I listened for footsteps outside and then slid the door open. I had to find Reegan. I had to know what this theory was.

I raced down the stairs, hoping he was down in the maintenance room. My training would have to wait. Consequences be damned. My thoughts raced along with my feet. Taking ever more strange and unwieldy paths to more and more illogical destinations.

By the time I came out of that spiral, I was at the archway to the engine room. Reegan stood just outside it with Jimman, speaking in whispers, their heads close together.

"Selah," Reegan said as I walked up.

"What's going on?" My voice was screechy, tense. I tried to take a deep breath to calm down and ended up coughing.

"Are you ok?" Jimman asked.

"Fine." I held a hand to my chest. "What's happening?"

"Nothing," Reegan said. "We're just making some plans. Did you get my note?"

"Yes."

That was all that came out. I wanted to say, *Do you think I'm sick? Why have you let me stay on the ship? Did I infect my father? What if he's dead? What if he caught the disease from me?* But none of it spilled out. I thought I might burst with the need to say it all, but I couldn't force my lips to open, my vocal chords to vibrate.

"Everything is ok." He put a hand on my shoulder and peered into my eyes. "Really. You're just fine. I only want to compare some things. We can discuss it later."

I thought my heart would pump itself right out of my chest and bounce along the floor until it was out of sight. He wanted me to wait? Now? When he had introduced all of these crazy ideas to my head?

"Shouldn't you be in training?" he asked. "Selah?"

"Yes." I turned and went upstairs. I imagined them watching me walk away, concern on their faces. In reality they probably went back to whatever they had been talking about. I wasn't as important as I thought I was. I couldn't be.

The training room was nearly empty when I got there. A few people remained—Kellan and Geric and the girls. They all focused on me when I entered.

"Galon left us to do one-on-one sparring." Geric's handsome face warmed into a smile.

I smiled back, then caught myself and fell back into a scowl. "And?"

"You're the only one left. You and Kellan. Have fun." He signaled the hologram to start as he and the girls walked out.

I faced Kellan. He was holding a weapon already with

one eyebrow raised. The room became a desert. Something that would physically tax us with the deep, sliding sand but where we wouldn't have to worry about touching plants or running into animals. Kellan tossed me a staff. It flew through the air, and my hand jumped up to meet it almost without me thinking. It smacked with a sting and a satisfying sound that reverberated around the room. Then a pair of goggles wacked me on the cheek. I growled at Kellan as I bent to pick them up. The walls were an endless sea of sand and blue sky. It had potential to let us wander forever in any random direction without fear of starvation or dehydration or sunburn. The holograms could be incredibly deceiving and made real life back at home seem like a particular cruelty.

Kellan took his stance. The hologram suddenly changed and produced large boulders scattered around the room. Neither of us had signaled for something different. I looked around for another person, and when I looked back, Kellan was gone, hiding somewhere in the boulder field. On the far wall, a sandstorm built in the distance. I would have to work fast.

I crouched low and went around boulder after boulder. I stretched one leg far in front of my body and slid forward to meet my foot, then dragged my rear leg to step forward again. Spreading my weight over the sand was easier on my vascular system, but it made for slow progress. Bent in half, I peered around a boulder and suddenly felt a whack on my back. I whipped around, my own staff at the ready, and lunged toward where Kellan should have been standing. He wasn't there. I looked to the top of the boulder to see if he had climbed it, but he wasn't there either.

The sky grew darker as I snuck around. Every now and

then, I felt the sting of plastic on skin. But I never saw Kellan and never got my own hit in. Passing around a particular boulder, I heard a laugh and lunged toward the sound. There was no one there. That's when I glanced up at the observation deck and saw a hand pressed against glass, floating in the sky. They could see me, but I couldn't see them. But it was glass, and they were stupid. Kellan was getting help.

I ran, slipping on the mounds of sand, to the door. There I signaled for the storm to manifest immediately. The room went nearly black, and wind buffeted me from all sides. I would have preferred to be without the sand stinging me in places I didn't know existed, but the dark was my element. My eyes were tuned to this. Even Kellan didn't have as good of eyesight in the dark as I did.

I stayed near the door, thinking he might try to make a break for it when he knew I had the advantage. After a few moments there was no sign of him, so I started a methodical search of the room. Maybe he was sheltering under one of the boulders and didn't want to risk his beautiful skin to the sand now swirling in the air, almost thick enough to choke and drown us.

I spotted a boulder a few feet away from the one I hid behind. It had a tiny overhang and what I thought might be a darker shadow than it should have. I circled around so I was coming at it from behind, and then I surveyed some more. There was definitely the shape of a leg, half-buried in the sand beneath the ledge on this boulder. I steadied myself against the rock. It felt scratchy and solid, just like a real rock should.

I waited another moment, ready for Kellan to be behind me or moving on the horizon. I wanted to be sure before I leapt.

A minuscule grunt came from below the boulder. I took up my staff like a spear and lunged forward, jabbing it into the space between rock and sand. The simulation absolutely disappeared. An alarm sounded, and Kellan lay at my feet on the floor of the holo-studio, a trickle of blood forming below his body.

Violence was forbidden.

I had injured him.

"You'll pay for this," he groaned, putting pressure on the wound.

I helped him stand and hung his free arm over my shoulder. "Come on. Let's get you to the med lab."

"Fuck you." He stumbled away from me.

The door opened, and his friends reached for him, pulling him into a group embrace and awkwardly trying to support him all at once. It turned into a mess of them carrying him. He wasn't nearly that badly hurt. I choked on a laugh as I watched them wobble down the hall.

Then that same laugh turned into a gasp as Galon stepped into view from the side of the door.

"I'm thinking that was a bad decision," he said.

"It was an accident. Besides, they were helping him against me. I thought the purpose was to spar one-on-one, not team-on-one?" I crossed my arms and cocked a foot.

"True. But your performance will need to be reviewed."

"Cool. Tell me what they find." I swept past him, making sure to jostle him as I did. I was so over putting up with him. I had just been attacked by the rest of my generation. Didn't that deserve a review as well? Where was the respect line drawn? Was I the only one held to any standards?

I thought I was free, but then his hand snagged my arm.

"I don't think you understand," he growled. "We're going to speak with Argana right now."

CHAPTER FOURTEEN

Argana approached me where I sat with Galon in the cafeteria. People parted around her, giving her plenty of berth. Like she was hot to the touch or carried the poisonous SE bacteria in her hands. In reality she was just walking. She even had a warm smile on her face. Through the crowd, I could tell she was headed directly for me. Her path led straight from the door to me, the fastest way from point A to point B.

"Hello, Selah." She eyed Galon. "Can we speak privately please?"

It was strange to see her without her henchmen. It made her seem taller. She took up more space than usual. She was actually more intimidating without her intimidators.

I stood and left my food but grabbed my water bottle. I didn't dare see what Galon's reaction was. It was likely that he had expected to be present for my thrashing. She took me to a table that was empty and far from other people. No one came near anyways because of the danger she radiated.

"I came to see you because we have some issues to address."

I nodded.

"I first want to make sure that you're doing ok. You can speak candidly with me. It's important to me that the subjects stay mentally and physically stable, so please feel free to tell me about anything that's troubling you." She thrust her hands onto the table and folded them together.

The buzz of the cafeteria seemed to fade out, but I was sure it was just my blood pressure rising to block the noise.

I took a sip of water. "Everything is fine."

She nodded slightly.

"Really." I looked at the ceiling, then cursed myself for giving away the lie.

"You're not worried about your father?"

"Of course I am," I snapped. I had to get control of myself. I bit the inside of my cheek before speaking again. "But there's not much I can do about it until you tell me where he is. So will you tell me?"

"He's currently in custody due to some strange findings he was hiding from the WHO. It was dangerous for him to do that. He was jeopardizing the entire project. He's safe. I can assure you."

I snorted.

"Is there anything else bothering you though? Your lashing out at Kellan seemed rather violent and rash. We want to ensure you're performing at your best."

"I would say my performance was pretty awesome. I won the spar against uneven odds."

"You mean the light being so low from the storm?"

"No. I mean the unfair advantage Kellan had by his friends watching from the observation deck and feeding him information on my whereabouts."

"We didn't notice that happening. I'll have someone look into it."

"I already mentioned it to Galon. I'm surprised he didn't inform you. Or maybe I'm not surprised. Kellan will be fine, yes?"

"He'll be ok in a few days. You're lucky you didn't puncture any organs." The concern on her face was intense. It seemed to leak out and force guilt and shame down my esophagus.

"That's ridiculous. It was a flesh wound. Those staffs are apparently too sharp. Maybe you should have that looked at." I took another sip of water. "Is there anything else? Can I go?"

"There are just a few other things."

I indicated she should continue with a sweep of my hand.

"Your contact with your mother has been monitored and will continue to be so. Your tablet, as well as any research on it, has been confiscated. Your disregard of my warning to not wander about the halls at random times has been noted. We will watch you more closely to be sure of your health and safety." She rattled all this off like a list of names on a roster, her voice steady and monotone.

I was pretty sure they hadn't discovered our room by the engines. Jimman deserved a hug when I was able to escape and see him again. They didn't have the journal. I took my time answering, forcing my voice to be as level as hers.

"That's all? I can go now?"

"You may go."

I stood from the table and gripped its edge to keep myself from wobbling. Then I commanded my legs to march, at least until I reached the safety of the hallway. Argana stayed seated, her eyes boring into my back like lasers as I left.

Through the door and around the corner, back against the wall and chest rising and falling rapidly with each breath, I tried to find something solid to focus on. Unfortunately it ended up being the person-shaped shadow coming toward me, which happened to materialize into Galon.

I groaned.

"You have been banished from the generation bunks, from the generation training, and from any generation activities."

"Great," I said.

"I don't like that tone. I've assigned you a solo bunk down the hall from us. You will still be required to train, but it will be personally, with me, at alternate times, in the smaller holo-studio."

I groaned again. That holo-studio was tiny enough to make me feel claustrophobic on a good day, let alone with Galon breathing the same oxygen and crowding me.

"You acted deplorably toward Kellan, and this is your punishment," he continued. And I knew the words had been fed to him, because when had Galon ever contorted his lips around a word like "deplorably"? Plus, how was isolation from my tormentors a punishment?

I wouldn't voice my opinion on that in case he caught on and realized a bigger punishment would be to tie me to Kellan's side for twenty-four hours. I kept my mouth shut and waited for the torture to be over.

"Well then," he said. "Ok." And he walked away.

I let out the breath I had been holding but kept hold of the tears. I needed somewhere much more private to let those fall.

I found myself sprinting once again, this time up the stairs to find Reegan in the labs. By the time I reached the windows of one of the main labs, with a view of screens and tables and blue-ish light from the machines and cords zig-zagging everywhere, I was out of breath. I collided with a guard standing in front of the door. It felt like hitting a concrete wall, he was so solid. I peeked around him and realized I had also been somehow surpassed by Argana. She was inside in a meeting with the scientists. Her back was to me, but Reegan caught my eye and shook his head at me. I backed slowly away as I smiled at the concrete wall in the black tunic until I was out of sight. I waited for a moment, pondering and catching my breath. Was there a way to listen in on that conversation?

Then I remembered the room-to-room intercall system I had seen my father use. So I went to his lab and located the main control panel. It wasn't hard to figure out how to listen to the other room—I only worried they would hear me start the call. But after I ignored my fears and hit the button anyway, the yelling that came through probably covered any beep or noise the system had made.

"It's unacceptable," Argana shouted. "To let this kind of information leak through. It's absolutely unacceptable. You will reinforce security and learn to keep your mouths shut."

"I'm sorry," a man's voice said. "It slipped through in the report to the UN."

The slap of a hand on a metal table rang through.

"The UN doesn't care or need to know. All they need to know is that we are working our hardest to make this happen. Don't be so stupid please."

"It won't happen again. I assure you."

"No. It won't. Because you won't be finding that we are stagnating again. You will work day and night to make sure we begin evolving. You will assure that your brains do what they were hired to do and create a new strain of human DNA that will make progress. That is why this won't happen again. Not because you mindlessly included information on a report that wasn't necessary."

The click of her heels filled the speaker, and then a door slammed. The scientists began murmuring, but so many of them were talking that I couldn't distinguish much. I turned off the call.

My face sufficiently puffy, my body dehydrated from the loss of fluids, and my throat a little bit sore from sobbing it raw, I sat up. Then I went for a walk. I circled the entire science level, avoiding the labs and their giant windows. I didn't really register more than the gray of the metal, the clang of random doors, the brisk gust of air whenever I passed a crossroads or open passageway.

I went into the stairwell by habit and went down two levels. I wandered in a straight line through the main hallway, passing by the cafeteria—noisy with children. I dawdled by an observation window to the holo-studio, which was occupied so I kept going, slowing at the stairs again and going down to enter the comms room once I realized it was empty.

Argana had said they were watching my conversations with my mother. They had taken my tablet, but could I still communicate with her? The last life-line to my sanity, I felt. If this didn't work, I might just hang myself from the rafters by the string in my pants.

When the screen came to life, a message started playing before I was allowed to log in.

It was a simple video. One that made this ship look so pretty, like paradise. It didn't feel like paradise.

"The modification project is an incredible feat of scientific engineering." The voice-over cut in as the video moved from the outside of the gleaming ship (which in reality was pretty rusty and pockmarked from sandstorms) down through the holo-studio solarglass onto a generation of modified going through their calisthenics.

"These children were bio-engineered to be better, faster, and more capable of handling our environment. The end idea is to jump-start evolution in a new generation of humans. We hope that by testing our subjects in different environments and scenarios, we will force their genetics to begin the work of evolution and continue our species."

It was propaganda. I finally saw it for what it was. The "updates" that weren't entirely truthful from the UN. This message we were required to watch before being allowed into a system that was being monitored. I had never known it before, but now I was awake. I was used to control. My day-to-day life was built out of control and monitoring and specifications. But it went far beyond that. The wider world was being controlled without their consent. Did my mother know this? Had I just been naive? Or was this a secret from the public? Was this possibly the secret my father had found?

It couldn't be. This had nothing to do with me specifically. But it certainly wasn't a good secret.

I opened a typed message and started a letter to my mother. I couldn't be as transparent as before, but I would get the message across.

Mother,

How are things in the city? I've heard something here that is good news. I'll tell you all about it when I've got a chance to record a hologram. Just know that Bearna's brother's owner is safe.

Besides that, I'm wondering something. You know how isolating the ship can be, how small of a world it can become. So I'm wondering if you can give me a long hologram on your thoughts about our world today. I'm assigning you an essay of sorts. Hopefully that will help me live vicariously through you and experience it all from your view. Your personal view.

I love you.

Selah

I read it three times, checking and checking again from every possible perspective. I assumed Bearna's name was not known as she had never been near any of the people on the ship, so they would have never heard us call her name. I also assumed they would see this as a plea for "home" and the feelings surrounding all of that instead of a quest for the political climate of the public. My finger still shook as I signaled the screen to send.

Message failed, the screen read in bright red.

I knew I had given the correct command. I tried again.

Message failed and erased.

"What?" I screamed. "I can't believe this. There must be a storm."

I shoved back from the table and stood.

There was one last thing to try. One last hope. I dashed out of the room and down to my secret room. I grabbed Rusty and typed frantically.

Can this send more than one liners? Could I send files? Can I say anything I want to? How protected is this?

I sent the message to my uncle and didn't get a response for the ten minutes I was able to sit still and wait. My patience ran out, so I walked out into the hallway, only to be met by Darm. I jumped in place, my hand to my heart.

"Come with me," he said.

I followed him to a room with a bunk and a table and chair. He held the door open.

"I'll be right outside if you need anything," he said.

My imprisonment had begun. I hadn't heeded Argana's warnings, and now I would have a leech by my side. I could only do as he said and hope Reegan figured out what was going on.

I went to the center of the tiny room. The door slammed behind me. The synthetic floor beneath my feet supported me well, but the fear and stress sent my soul plummeting through every level below me and into the sand.

CHAPTER FIFTEEN

My father was gone. Supposedly alive and safe, but gone. My mother was unreachable, held captive by my overlords using the simple tactic of not allowing communication. My patience was being tested by forcing me into solitary confinement and training with the one person who possibly outright hated me. I was very probably a twin and so felt an explanation for the constant hole in my heart but had nothing more than that explanation to fill it.

I continued to question my identity and whether or not I truly belonged to the parents who had given me half of their genetic code upon conception—half of which was changed to artificial code only two weeks after said conception. I hadn't heard back from my uncle and feared the worst for him. What else did I have to turn to?

The lights came on in the holo-studio, and the older generation started filing in, filtering around me like the hills of sand that were drowning me in sorrow. I left, saw Darm standing guard in the hall, and entered the door next to the holo-studio, the smaller one. While I didn't normally like this room with its low ceiling and constant smell of sweat, at this moment, it felt cozy and secluded. Plus I knew I would be left alone because no one else wanted to voluntarily practice in here. People would head to the observation decks on the top of the ship where it was cold and overly bright and all metal and glass before they would work in here. Here there were no windows. If I left the light off, I was in complete darkness. I didn't want to feel quite that lost, so I set the lights low.

I swept my body through flowing movement, allowing my muscle-memory to take control. One arm flashed through the air around me, swinging my body with its momentum. A leg came up and stepped forward with a lunge, but nothing was jerky or loud. I controlled my foot and set it down gingerly. I bent my body in half and brought the top half through like a snake, head first. Then I let my other arm float forward to meet and started a new form, stepping my other leg to meet and then to the side.

The door clicked, the only sound alerting me to someone's presence. The hairs on my neck stood on end, and I shivered. I flipped around to face a shadow in the corner.

"Hello." Galon stepped into a halo of dim light.

I nodded.

"Your training session will begin now. Do you need water first?"

I nodded again and walked to take a bottle from his hands. He held onto it for a second before grinning and letting go. After I took a sip and set the bottle down, he started meandering around the perimeter of the room and calling out instruction for a series of flowing poses. I pushed my muscles through, ignored my elevated heartbeat, and regulated my breathing to match my pace.

"Do that for five more rounds," he said.

And I did, while he talked. I couldn't quiet my mind and drown out his voice in this tiny place. So I let him unload his diatribe.

"This world began with nature, and it will end with nature. We humans think we have control of things. No, we *wish* we had control of things. It has ruined my faith in my own species. We are ridiculous. We couldn't have done better if we had created the SE bacteria ourselves."

At this point he started mumbling to himself, and I was able to shut him off for a bit. But the volume of his voice only grew until I could no longer ignore him. "It's exactly what we deserve. We are cruel creatures, and there is no reason we shouldn't be wiped from existence in a cruel way. This world will come to an end, Selah." He turned to face me.

I stopped moving through the motions, my arms limp by my sides.

"It will be our fault. But that is the way it should be. Mark my words. Your father and the WHO and everyone will get what's coming to them. Even I am not afraid to die, because I know that's what nature has planned for me, whether it's because of old age or because my body is being punished for the sins of our forefathers—I will die, and I will be happy to see the rest of our species taken down with me."

He was nuts. Completely and absolutely. I wouldn't have been surprised to find out he was going to blow up the ship or something else drastic. He turned around and swept from the room.

I backed up into the holo-studio and let the quiet calm my nervous system. My heart was no longer racing. I knew what needed to be done.

I walked calmly into the hallway. Darm turned to face me.

"I need to speak with Argana," I said.

He nodded and led the way to the science level. There we found her speaking with some of the scientists. We waited. The scientists left, and we still waited. Argana worked on her tablet. I cleared my throat. She didn't look up. When I felt like giving up, she finally lifted her head and smiled at me.

"What can I do for you, Selah?"

I glanced at Darm and spoke.

"Galon is a rebel."

Silence.

"He was spouting rebel ideologies at me today, and he has before."

"And you didn't report it before because?" She folded her hands together on the table before her.

"It has reached a new level. Today he was talking about nature and people dying and how controlling the natural order is dangerous for human kind."

"I see. Well, thank you for telling me."

She went back to her work on her tablet.

"You're not going to do anything?" I rushed forward, slamming my hands on the table. "He could be a danger to this entire ship!"

She didn't raise her head, simply spoke while typing something. "My brother is a danger to no one, believe me."

I leaned into the table, my jaw dropping open.

"He's a harmless little fly. That said, you will still obey him. His orders come from me, and mine come from the WHO. You are contracted to work for us until we deem your contract no longer necessary. Thank you for the information,

Selah." She waved her hand at the air, and Darm pulled me from the room.

I don't know how much time passed. I only know my body was glistening with sweat when Reegan opened the door to the smaller holo-studio. He stepped inside, closed the door, and I crumpled to the floor in a heap.

I felt his arms around me, at first just holding me and then pulling me up onto his lap. Tears poured down my face. Sound did not escape me, simply because I was so completely exhausted.

"My sweet Selah. What happened?"

I told him everything. I told him about Argana and Galon, about the failed letter to my mother, about my realization that our world was under the thumb of people we shouldn't trust. And I expressed my fears that I was less my parent's child than a child of science.

He listened, and then he said, "You are alone. There is no one in this world that can possibly fulfill your needs other than yourself." In the pause between his words I felt that I had possibly lost the last person in this world who could help me. But then he continued. "But Selah, you are loved. You know this, and you need to acknowledge it. This idea that you don't belong to your parents is complete bullshit. Your mother carried you inside her body and gave birth to you. The focus of your life has been about the science, but your father has kept a particular eye on you and obviously ran more experiments on your birth than any other baby. Doesn't that prove to you that he, of all people, wanted his own child to succeed? To live?"

I couldn't bring myself to look at him.

"I have a plan," Reegan said.

"Is it to go to Argana's office with a bucket of acid and a knife so I can burn her face off and then stab her?"

Reegan pulled back from me a little. The silence was palpable.

"Sorry. I have no idea where that came from. I'm really not a violent person," I said.

He put a hand to my cheek.

"The plan is to send the ship toward the jungle, get off so I can get a sample, get back on so I can study it in the lab, and compare it to your DNA strand."

"You're nuts. None of that will work. And why?" I swallowed and found the courage to say what I hadn't been able to say in my confession. "Do you think I'm a carrier?"

"Not at all!"

"Then what?" I jumped to my feet, too agitated to stay curled up in his lap, gazing up at him like some soppy puppy.

"I think you're immune."

If I thought the failed message to my mother had sent me through the floor, this statement was like a building crashing down on top of me *after* I fell through the floor and six feet into the sand.

"I think your father hypothesized that you were immune to SE. I think you and your twin were different because you split the modification between you."

"But that would mean the whole system is working toward the wrong goal."

"Not really. We still need to evolve. But if we could introduce immunity, life would be a hell of a lot easier."

"What do we do?"

"We run the ship into the jungle and prove the theory. I need fresh SE bacteria in its current form. The DNA strands we have in the archives are too old. Your father will have already tested against them. The only problem I have is how we get past Argana to tell the right people."

"I might have the answer to that," I said. "But we have to get away from my bodyguard."

Reegan took my hand and pulled me into the hallway.

"I need to run some tests on Selah," he told Darm. "I'll bring her back to your care when we're finished."

He cut off Darm's answer by walking away. I peeked back to see Darm shaking his head and rocking on his feet, unsure of whose orders to follow. But we turned a corner, and he didn't seem to be following us. I squeezed Reegan's hand tighter and ran with him to my secret room.

I took a deep breath before turning Rusty on, really hoping to hear that chirp. I closed my eyes and waited.

I was rewarded. It chirped after a few minutes of being powered. Reegan tilted his head at me. I crooked one side of my lips up and opened the message.

You can do whatever you wish. This is a freedom-filled zone. No one has this network but us, and no one would even consider hacking it because they don't imagine it's there. I'm on an old cell satellite. It might have slow upload speeds, but you can send files. Those satellites haven't been serviced in years, so they're rusty. ;) -T

"What's that semi-colon and parenthesis?" I pointed the screen at Reegan.

His eyes got wider the more of the message he consumed.

"It's an emoticon."

"Huh?" I turned Rusty back to look at it again.

"An old way of building smiley faces in text. What is this?" He took it from me.

"You know Tobias. He's crazy. But he's also a genius."

CHAPTER SIXTEEN

If we had been sneaking before, now we were in true stealth mode. If someone saw us on the way to the navigation system, we were screwed. So we moved from shadow to shadow, taking our time down each hallway and at each corner. Our combined years of training came in handy. We became part of the ship.

Out of the corner of my eye I spotted a camera in the ceiling. The red blinking light wasn't blinking. I stopped to stare.

"Reegan?"

"Yeah?"

I pointed.

"Ah. No worries. Before I came to get you I had Jimman shut off the camera system and the first level of fail-safes."

"What?"

"How else were we supposed to accomplish this?"

"I had no idea he had access to that."

"Technically he doesn't. But he understood the urgency of the situation. He also helped me out with some access hatches and other ways around the ship."

"Ways that I don't know?"

Reegan's lip curled up on one side. "Ways that even you don't know."

The navigation room, as I knew from my other wanderings, was locked. But Reegan had been speaking with Jimman and the other maintenance workers for a reason.

"There's a code," he whispered. "Unfortunately I couldn't get my hands on the actual code."

"But if it's a code instead of a key, it can be hacked." I rubbed my hands together. This was exciting.

"Precisely." He pulled at the panel next to the door. Throughout the ship, the walls randomly opened to reveal access to wiring and duct work and anything needing maintenance. That included any computer panels like the hologram creator in the holo-studio or the wallscreens in the cafeteria. As well as the screen outside the navigation room which took a code to open. Reegan set to work at the back of the computer, plugging his own tablet in and scrolling through lines of code.

"Eureka!"

"Shush!" I put my hand over his mouth.

He snickered. Of course he did. Then I did too.

The door popped off its lock and fell open an inch. I checked both directions for anyone coming and squeezed in. Reegan came in behind me but didn't close the door all the way.

"What are you doing? What if someone comes?"

"And what if the hacked system gets pissed and locks us inside? I'd rather not take that chance. Maybe getting caught versus definitely getting caught—I prefer the risk of someone walking by."

"Makes sense. Now what?" I turned to see what I hadn't

seen yet—a wall of blinking lights and a giant screen running calculations. Reegan's jaw dropped open. "You didn't get this far in your talks with Jimman?" I teased.

"No, not really. Jimman doesn't actually have access to this room."

"And he couldn't get it?"

"He got me the code, didn't he?"

I assessed the situation logically. We knew this computer navigated the ship. Did it do anything else—like control the hovering or the metal shields that protected the body during a storm? If it did, we would need to first find the navigation system.

"What all does this computer do?"

"Hell if I know." Reegan threw his hands in the air.

"Seriously? This is as far as your plan got? Into the room?"

"I got us that far, didn't I?"

"Great."

I stepped up to the screen and tried to follow the rapid calculations. They were much too fast, so I put a finger out to touch the screen. Reegan slapped it down.

"What are you doing?"

"We have to do something. If I can tell what the calculations are doing, I can tell if this system does more than navigating. If it only navigates, then I need to figure out where we are and where the jungle is and how to get there, and do you not understand what a mess you've gotten us into?"

"I'm sorry. Proceed." He stepped back to face the wall and bang his head.

"Stop. Someone will hear you." I studied the blinking lights.

"I hit my head and you tell me to stop because someone might hear me. If I didn't know you so well, I'd think you didn't love me."

"Shut up."

He did. And I touched my finger to the screen. The calculations slowed enough for me to read them, but no alarm sounded. We both sighed.

"These are definitely navigation calculations."

"How can you tell?" He joined me in bending close to the screen.

"See the coordinates? Those are the answers to the previous calculations and used in the ones after them."

"Ok, but do you see how it's navigating us?" He pointed to one of the coordinates and then the next. "It's making tiny calculations. Like minuscule. How will we ever force it a certain direction?"

"There has to be an end destination and parameters. That means we can ignore the parameters because we don't care if we hit the jungle, and we can choose the jungle as our end destination."

"Oh. That's so good, Selah."

"Thank you."

"No!" I jumped at his cry. "All we have to do is cut out the parameters. The ship will get stuck in the jungle, so if we command that it doesn't have to avoid it, we'll eventually hit it."

"Won't that take ages? What if we're miles from it?"

"Ah, now that is something Jimman knows." He started strutting around the room with one hand behind his back and the other gesturing in the air. "The ship is run parallel to the jungle so we can utilize the moisture to create our water supply. It also protects us from some of the worst sandstorms."

"It's still possible we won't run into the jungle. If the sand has successfully kept the jungle at bay, and we continue straight, there's high probability that we won't run into it."

"We'll turn left a little?" His eyebrows rose with the pitch of his voice.

"Are you kidding? How did they ever let you into a science lab?"

"I wonder if we could see the jungle from the observation decks."

"Again, what idiot let you touch science experiments?"

"Your father."

The mood, which had been a mixture of light and playful with stress and urgency, stopped dead. The hum of the engines, only a few walls away from us, penetrated our eardrums. Then so did the faintest clang of steps.

Reegan lunged for the door, peeked through, then gently pressed it closed. We both waited for the alarm, for the beep that said the door was now permanently locked, for something to happen. Nothing did.

"Look, I'm apparently not taking this seriously—"

"You think?" I spat.

"Ok. Let's reassess what we know. We know this computer controls navigation only. We know the calculations are tiny, so easily interrupted, but for how long? And we know that there must be parameters set to keep the ship away from the jungle while also heading for an ultimate destination. So what's the final stop?"

"We know we get on at the shipyards and back off at the same place."

"And we know we have to keep moving to keep the ship safe as well as functioning since half of its systems require moisture and wind."

"Are we just going in circles?"

"That would be the most logical. Then no one has to set a destination at all. The destination is always the port. They just point the ship to the side at the beginning of the summer and face the dock again at the end of the summer, other than that, it just goes around to the dock and resets when we reach it to go in another circle."

"Can we tell which direction we're going from the coordinates?"

We glued our faces to the screen again, our brains working a mile a minute. I paused during my search to study the line of stubble on Reegan's cheek and listen for anything out of the ordinary. Whoever was out walking the halls hadn't come any closer to us, yet.

"There. I recognize that number," Reegan said.

"You do?"

"I got bored this last winter. I spent a lot of time looking at maps and determining what the world used to look like. I know where the port is, and that number is it. We must be coming close to it."

"The day we leave from port, the sun rises from the east side of the ship in our direction of travel. I watch it from the holo-studio every year."

"The sun!" Reegan slapped a hand over his mouth. We both went to the door and put our ears against it. Nothing.

"What about it?" I whispered.

"Why did I never think of that fact that it changes its position as we travel? I feel like such an idiot."

I pinched my lips together, holding the words in.

"Still doesn't solve which direction we're going. If we send ourselves through the center of the circle, we risk driving straight into the desert."

"No we don't," Reegan said. His face lit up like a wallscreen come to life.

It dawned on me. We were traveling in a circle. We also had to stay close to the jungle for moisture. We were in a circular desert. If we sent the ship off course, it didn't matter which way we went. It might take longer one way or the other, but in the end we would reach the jungle.

"Oh," I said. "One last problem."

"Yep?" Reegan plugged his tablet into the console and started working through some lower level programs.

"What if the crash is catastrophic? What if people get hurt?"

"It's a hovership. It'll stop when it can't hover anymore. And it's made of steel. We'll be fine."

I went back to the door to test if it would open—it did. There was no one in the hall. Our luck was holding, but my nerves tingled, and my adrenaline levels were reaching their max.

"Can you hurry at all?" I asked.

"I think I found the file. Come look at this."

I peered over his shoulder and saw that he was into the basic code of the computer. From what I could read of the few lines visible, it looked like we were right on all counts.

"That one." I pointed.

"Yep."

One line directed to an entire folder of files. He found the folder and moved it to his tablet, then deleted it from the navigation computer entirely. That was the moment I was happy I had propped the door again because the walls burned red and an alarm blared so loud my head wanted to split open.

CHAPTER SEVENTEEN

We ran without checking for observers. The hallway was empty, bathed in red, and vibrating. The metal made the perfect sounding board. Reegan kept going down the hallway, but I skidded to a stop and reversed. I went back and put the panel for the code lock back together and into the wall. Then I shut the door and waited for the click of the lock. The alarm stopped.

"Interesting," I said to myself.

We were still off course, so the alarm should have continued. It wasn't as if we had broken into the room and then the alarm started. It hadn't begun blaring until after we removed the files.

I stumbled as I tried to turn the right direction and caught up to Reegan.

"They'll know where the alarm originated," he said.

"But why did it turn off? What if the ship is still on course? What if it fixed itself?"

"Hopefully that's not the case. Keep running. We can't get caught here."

We flew up two flights of stairs and stopped for a breather. On floor five, we dashed to the secret room, and I grabbed Rusty. Then it was straight back to the stairs, but one floor up, at the modified level, I stopped.

"What's up?" he asked.

"I need to go look at something."

"I'll come with you. I don't want you going alone."

So instead of climbing more stairs, we went into the hallway. There weren't many people around. They were probably mostly on the observation deck already, ever since the alarm went off. I led Reegan down the hall to my generation's sleeping room.

I went directly to my locker, where I had left some things when I was moved to my punishment bunker, and felt around for my work bag. It lay at the bottom, in a heap. I hadn't been using it much. I pulled my mother's scarf from the bag. With it came a flutter of paper. While I wrapped the scarf around my neck, Reegan bent to the pick up the paper.

"This is a note from your father."

I stopped inhaling the scent of my mother and looked at the paper as he held it out to me. It was ciphered, but only our simple code. It was easy for both of us to read even if it seemed too simple and obvious.

Check the false panel in your locker.

"Really?" Reegan said.

He reached into the locker, pulled the rest of the stuff out, and then felt around inside. Something clicked, loudly. Then he pulled out a sheaf of paperwork.

Geric walked into the room right then. I took the paperwork and shoved it into my work bag and tossed the rest of my belongings back into my locker, hiding the false panel.

"Hi," I said. And I dragged Reegan from the room.

Walking up the next flight, we encountered Galon. That lovely specimen of a human stood in front of us with a smug grin on his face. The man I had known only three years previously didn't seem to exist anymore. His eyes were harder, more squinted. His cheeks were sunken. He radiated frustration and anger.

"Where is your guard?" he said, circling us.

"I have custody of her for now," Reegan said.

"And yet you aren't anywhere near your area of expertise." He sniffed as if catching the scent of where we had been, what we were up to.

"I've just retrieved her. We're going upstairs. I don't need to answer you. What am I doing?"

As Reegan pulled me past him, I glanced back, hoping for a glimpse of the person I once knew. I was disappointed when he growled at me and flared his lips. Reegan continued to drag me, and Galon laughed, his head thrown back in exaggeration as he walked down the stairs.

"Ignore him. He can't do anything, even if he figures out what we were doing. Argana is the one we want to worry about. Let me know if you see her. We need to gather some supplies."

I started running in earnest again, my heart left behind at the previous staircase, next to the ghost of a man I had once known.

We made it up two more flights of stairs and onto the lab level. Reegan ran from room to room like he was on fire. He grabbed two or three things from one room, shoved them into my arms, and went into another room. He came out bearing more gifts and then gestured me into the largest lab. There I set everything down on the table in front of me and waited for him to find his bearings. He whipped this way and that, not really grabbing things, mostly just picking things up and putting them back down. A few he even picked up again.

"Reegan. Focus."

"Sorry. This is difficult. I've never done a pull from the real world."

"What do we need?"

"A lot. Everything? Can we just bring the whole lab?"

"Sorry. Probably not." I sifted through the things on the table he had set down—some tubing, a few random syringes, a flashlight, a probe, scissors. "What is all this? You've studied the texts. Even if you haven't done it in person, you know what to do. So think!"

I swept the stuff off the table and threw a bag on top. Then I went over and stood in front of him to wait for his brain to catch up.

"We need suits. A sampler. And those pliers over there." He went to work, listing off things for me to find and tossing things on the table near the bag.

When we had a mound that I couldn't see over, I started placing it all carefully in the bag. There weren't many sensitive instruments as we would use that kind of equipment when we got back on the ship. This trip was purely to gather the specimen. It meant using all of our training to avoid touching the plants even though we would be wearing the protective gear. It meant venturing far enough into the jungle to find plants that were most likely infected, but keeping the ship in sight so we didn't get lost. I bent down below the table and threw the flashlight in just in case.

"Selah."

"Yeah?" The tremor in his voice startled me. I came up slowly from behind the table, expecting Argana or someone at the door. There was no one in the room with us. "What's up?"

"How do we get off the ship? No. Sorry. I know how we open the doors and all that, but what if the plank won't go down in a safe spot on the jungle?"

My heart thudded into my feet. Reegan had come to me with a plan that was pockmarked and scarred. But my spirits lifted as my brain went to work. This was where I came in.

"That's not a problem at all. I can get us down."

Realization glowed on his face.

"No," he said. "I don't do heights. I don't solo like you."

"It's easy on the outside of the ship. There are levels to pause at and plenty of handholds. In fact, this is probably good because it's unlikely anyone will follow us if they have to climb down the side of the ship. It does curve a bit. I love that kind of challenge." I smiled, imagining the grip my fingers would have and the strain on my forearms, the burn in my toes.

"No. I can't do that."

I walked over to him and put my hands on his shoulders. I held his gaze steady on me.

"I'll help you every step of the way. I know how to do this. I can help you. We can make it to the sand easily. Then all we have to do is head into the jungle, and then it's up to you." My mind kept buzzing and whirring. "And then we'll climb back up. We can get around to the far side without being seen, where no one will be looking. Then we can walk over the top of the ship back to the door."

His shoulders rose and fell with shallow, stressed breaths.

"Reegan. Breathe. The ship isn't that tall. It'll take us fifteen minutes tops. I promise. You're strong enough."

He nodded.

I squeezed him and let go.

"We don't have to come back in the main door," he said. "Jimman told me about an access hatch on the roof."

"Why don't we leave that way?"

"Because it won't open from the inside without failure of the main door. It is accessible from the outside once the main door is open to the elements."

"Then we still have to use the main door, but we still have to climb back up to reach the access. I know you can do it, Reegan."

He nodded again.

We gathered the last few things and headed out of the lab. There was no knowing when the ship would hit the jungle, so we went to the observation decks, where everyone would probably be anyways.

***

"I really hope there's no one around the entrance doors," Reegan mused as we climbed more staircases.

"They'll be fascinated by the scene out the windows. It won't matter what we're doing. Even if they do see us."

"I hope so. It would really ruin all of this to get stopped now."

"I think it would be bad to get stopped at any point, but whatever you want to think." I shoved him playfully.

He tagged me and raced away. I chased after him, and we came to the top of the stairs, to the observation deck, where even with a vaulted ceiling and glass dome, a crowd of people loomed ominously. At the beginning of every summer, the crowd seemed tiny compared to the massive, rusty ship with sand stretching for days in each direction, but on the inside of the ship, this relatively small group overpowered the room.

Reegan and I made our way through, holding tight to each other's hands. Reegan wore the bag with sampling supplies over his shoulder. I gripped him like it was life or death. We came up to the glass to hopefully get a chance to see where the ship was headed. He pulled me to a metal joist, and we sat down with our backs to it, our legs stretched out on the floor, the mob pushing in around us like a giant sea. I pulled my bag onto my lap. The joist gave us sufficient protection and also allowed us to watch through the windows at the other sea outside, the sea of sand.

"How long do you think?" I was getting jittery, shifting in my seat and stretching my muscles randomly to let out the excess energy. I never liked waiting.

"There's no way to tell. I'm mostly worried about getting back to the lab once we've gotten back on the ship."

"We're highly trained deadly assassins, Reegan. Not a worry in the world." I winked and slapped my knee when it started bouncing of its own accord.

"All right then. We'll ninja our way through. But my main question is: what if someone follows us into the jungle?"

"Unlikely," I said. "They wouldn't want to risk exposure. Unless—"

We heard yelling in another part of the room. The sea of people shifted and undulated and then parted. I caught a view of Argana and some of her cronies marching through. I yanked my legs back, and Reegan followed suit. We made ourselves small, hidden inside the joist. The crowd covered any view of us. But I did see, through the forest of feet, heels on Argana's tiny feet. She was the only one who would bother wearing heels on a ship made of metal. I wondered how she navigated the staircases. Did her bodyguards carry her? Did she go barefoot? Did she risk breaking a shoe and just go for it?

The heels turned and went the other direction, and then I lost sight of them. At that moment, the crowd, which had been buzzing with whispers and talking, quieted. Reegan tapped me on the shoulder.

We both looked out the window, where the group of heads collectively turned. The horizon was the faintest shade of green. Like a painting with a sunset, the sea of sand melded into a line of green that glowed above the horizon and bled into the blue sky above.

Reegan stood and helped me to my feet, and we both crouched down as we pushed through the crowd. Finally, we were moving, and my nerves turned their anxiety into action. My muscles went to work at bending and twisting through the people. It was good practice for the jungle to come.

We came upon the entrance door. In the room made of glass, it was a large, round door the size of a bus at the end of a short passageway. No one was in the passageway, and we didn't want to try to hide in such an open space, so we settled in next to it, against the wall, half sitting with our backs pressed into the glass. The crowd again covered us, but I still stressed that Argana would think to come to the door.

Everyone was on the observation deck because it was the best place to see, but would Argana and the others think that someone had changed the navigation of the ship on purpose in order to get out? Who in their right minds would try to leave the ship? What were we doing?

My knee started bouncing up and down again. Reegan's hand came down and held me still.

"Let me do it," I said. "Movement helps."

"Don't be anxious," he whispered in my ear. "I'm here. This is the right thing to do. We'll be ok."

"Funny you say that. You must not be thinking about what happens after the door."

His face went white, and I cursed myself for reminding him.

CHAPTER EIGHTEEN

An alarm started up again somewhere. Red lights on the ceiling blinked to life. The room wasn't bathed in light like below, but there was a distinct hue to the faces and arms. I craned my head around to see out of the glass, and my jaw dropped.

"Reegan, look."

It was the most beautiful thing I had ever seen. It was paradise. A line of green that met the sand and curled over it like a hand reaching out. The fronds of the trees were soft and inviting. The deep dark between the trunks of the trees called to me. I wanted to disappear inside.

The ship didn't grind to a halt, or stop itself at all, it just kept going until it couldn't go anymore. The hovering cushion had allowed it to coast over the smaller vegetation. But it could only push so far, so the crowd nearly fell over from the force of the powerful engines trying to hover over ground that was no longer hoverable.

Reegan kept his balance and steadied me. We sprinted for the control panel next to the door. He plugged his tablet in and set to work. I looked back at the crowd, tapping my fingers on the wall in panic. There was no sign of Argana or anyone else that had their eyes on us. Reegan had been right—they were all glued to the windows.

But then the door popped open with a piercing hiss. All heads turned to face us. Their eyes wide. They were terrified of what might come in, now that the door was open. They weren't ready, even though I was.

Reegan and I slipped out before the door finished opening and then immediately turned around to close it. I saw Argana cutting a path through the crowd until the metal broke all contact with what we knew.

"Here we go," Reegan said.

He pulled our suits out, and we wiggled them on. Once the hoods were pulled up and zipped shut, the material tightened even more against our bodies, creating a second skin which we could feel through but which protected us from the elements. Then we entered the decontamination chamber for a spray shower.

We stood on the plank as it slowly pushed itself out into nothingness, reaching for a scaffold that wasn't there. He gulped and grabbed for me. I went to the side of the plank and crept out onto a ledge the size of half of my foot. I looked down at the sand, eleven floors below, and smiled. This was going to be amazing.

The wind pushed at my hair, inviting me to make the climb.

I took a deep breath. The smell hit me. It was fresh. And beautiful. And incredible. And suddenly Reegan screamed.

"What?" I looked at him.

He was clambering at the wall behind us. "I looked down."

"Ok. First step is to get to a ledge that's a little bit more than your height below us. We're going to the joist over here to use it. Stop looking down, and follow me."

We made it to the joist, where Reegan immediately clung onto both me and the extra metal. His fingers dug into my arm.

"That strength in your fingers, Reegan? That's exactly what you need. Place your hands where I place mine. We're going to face the ship so you can look at my hands or the wall."

I proceeded to place my fingers and feet where they needed to be. This wasn't going to be an easy solo climb by any means. It was a metal ship with slick sides, not a rock wall with divots and handholds. I focused my attention on placing my limbs properly. I didn't ignore Reegan, but I needed to find the right places first, then I could glance up and make sure he was following me step for step. When I had a moment, I glanced up toward the door just in case. I nearly fell from where I hung when I saw Galon in a suit, standing there, glaring at me.

"Fuck," I whispered.

"What?" Reegan screamed. "What?" He started faltering, looking at his hands and feet for something wrong, glancing around us in a panic. He was so freaked out that he never once looked up.

"It's nothing. Just keep going. Look at my hands." He didn't stop flicking his head around to find the source of my exclamation. "Reegan!" I yelled. "Pay attention. You don't want to lose grip here. Look at my hands. Place your hands. I'll get you down."

In the back of my mind, I was calculating the fastest way down as well as considering Galon's climbing abilities. I almost wished Argana had been standing there instead of him. She wouldn't have been able to even come out on the ledge, let alone follow us down to the sand below. Galon was the worst option. He was pretty decent when I had seen him climb. My brain calculated ever faster ways down, and I tried to think of ways to get him off our trail so he couldn't copy my path.

But then I realized that the more I worried about him, the slower I was going and the slower Reegan would go. I had to focus on Reegan.

We made it down two of the floors to a larger ledge, and I let Reegan rest. The green in front of us was becoming even more clear. I realized that the ship wasn't really sitting on sand, so our descent would be more difficult than I had thought. We had run so far into the jungle that there was only a small strip of sand before the trees. Some of the trees even brushed against the metal hull. One tree in particular, an old and obviously dead one, seemed outstretched just for my benefit. We could use it to climb down. Plus the sharp inversion of the last few stories would be easier if done on the tree instead of the ship.

I nudged Reegan and pointed to the tree. He had been sitting on the ledge, his knees pulled up and his head between his knees. He looked out and then down to the tree. He peered up at me like a little boy—horrified but hopeful.

I nodded.

He followed me down, even as the ship started to slant and our fingers started to shake. It was one of the most difficult climbs I had ever done, certainly the longest, and my muscles were screaming after the day of running and creeping we had already had. The adrenaline in my system was running out. Of course that sent me into another rush as I thought about all that lay ahead of us.

My foot hit something other than metal. It bent and moved away from me. I jumped.

It was the dead tree. I needed to pay better attention.

I reached for the wood and let my fingers graze it. Other than the artificial wood in the holo-studio, I had never felt wood before. It was smooth, warm, different. Even through the gloves, with their artificial touch, I knew it was something my body craved to be near.

I hopped out to the tree and clung to it. It swayed a little but stayed strong. I looked up at Reegan and happened to see Galon above him. He stood on the ledge we had rested on. He was a menacing sight above me like that. I shivered and then ignored him. I had to focus on getting Reegan down. The tree was still a good fifteen feet from the ground.

I scrambled down, and Reegan jumped out onto it. I heard a distinct crack. Reegan whimpered.

I went faster. Reegan stayed put.

"You have to keep coming. Staying still will only make it worse. You're very heavy on the top there. Come down just a little and then rest." He stayed put. "Please Reegan. I need you to scoot down just a few feet."

I got to the bottom of the tree and checked the ground for vegetation. Seeing a bare spot, I jumped down. I rolled my shoulders, feeling the burn. The base of the ship was solidly grounded on the scant vegetation at the edge of the sand. It wouldn't be hovering again anytime soon, and I could hear some ominous pops and hisses. Reegan was still at the top of the tree. I had to find a way to coax him down without actually climbing up there and putting more pressure on the creaking tree.

"There's a spider up above you!" I screamed.

Reegan gave up the fight, and he slid farther down the tree. Reegan glanced up, and instead of a spider, he saw Galon coming down over the ledge. He clambered the rest of the way down, his body clumsy and incapable of actually finishing the climb. He landed in a heap by my feet.

"We have to run." I bent down to help him up.

"How are we going to run? I can't feel my legs."

"Find the motivation inside you somewhere. If you don't, everything is lost. Without samples, this whole thing was pointless. Even if we can get back into the ship, we have to have the samples. So get up. Now." I hauled on him, forcing his body to an upright position. I swung one of his arms over my neck, and we limped together into the forest.

We ran into the jungle. The trees were bare enough here, probably from the sand blasting they consistently received, that we didn't have to dodge any leaves. But this also meant we would have to go farther than I really wanted to in order to find viable samples. We reached a clearing, and Reegan pulled me to the side. He crouched down.

I prompted him to drink from his reservoir, but then got him up and moving again.

I pushed Reegan harder to both get away from the sound of Galon behind us and to get closer to samples that would have living bacteria still inside.

He stumbled on a root, landed face first in a pile of dead sticks, and started screaming. I yanked him up.

"What's wrong?" I asked.

"Those sticks were eating me!"

"Get it together. Let's slow down."

The crashing behind us was definitely erratic, slowing to assess and then starting again with a vengeance. Galon had no idea where we were, and he had less capability in an environment like this. I started using that to our advantage by diving off into the undergrowth.

"Are you feeling better?" I asked.

Reegan nodded.

"Good. Because this is about to get harder."

We weaved through like two snakes slithering along. We kept as quiet as possible and disturbed as few leaves as we could. It seemed to be working because the sporadic thrashing behind us began to fade to our left.

"Can we take these leaves?" I whispered.

"I think we should go farther."

I looked back through the jungle and could just barely spot the ship through a triangle of foliage. It was quickly disappearing, and I wasn't certain how well I would be able to keep my bearings. While I looked back at the ship, I heard voices calling.

"Go," I whispered so hard my voice cracked and my throat hurt.

Reegan crawled on, perfectly in control of his body, though I could see slight tremors in his legs when he bent at a particularly difficult angle.

I slid through the brush behind him and came to another clearing. In front of us stood a very startled jaguar. Reegan was frozen. The jaguar had been in the midst of a meal, though its head was now raised, blood dripping from its jaw. And just as I pulled on Reegan's suit to get him to back away slowly, Galon came barreling into the clearing from another side. This startled the cat even more, and it leapt up into a tree and disappeared from view.

We all three stood locked in our positions, unable to move or think.

"We should leave. He'll want that back." I gestured at the half-eaten animal on the jungle floor.

I tried to use the moment of pause to pull Reegan away from Galon, but he was too slow. Galon lunged and tackled him. They rolled around on the leaves and branches that blanketed the ground. They were so fast that I had no chance to jump in. I just watched and hissed and cringed each and every time they made contact with green. I waited for the rip of fabric from one of their suits.

Their tussle slowed, due to their bodies being completely exhausted from the climb and the run, and I was able to wrench Galon's arm behind his back. I pulled him up, him screaming bloody murder like a little girl the whole time. Reegan lay on his back, panting.

"How about you leave us alone?" I said, my face close to Galon's, close enough that I could smell his sweat.

"What are you doing?" he managed through gritted teeth and groans.

"What do you think we're doing?"

"Enough with the questions." Reegan stumbled to his knees. Bright red blood streamed down his chin behind his protective hood.

Galon swung his other arm at me. I caught it and pinned it too behind his back.

"I have a little something for you, Galon," Reegan said. "I'm very sorry, but this might mean that you don't make it back onto the ship."

He strode over, flipped a cap off a tiny bottle, unzipped and peeled back Galon's headpiece, held his nose, and forced the contents down his gullet. He hacked and gurgled but drank it. It only took a few seconds before his system felt the effects, and I let go of his arms as he fell.

"Reegan!"

"What else could I do? We had to get him off us somehow." Reegan tugged Galon's hood back into place.

"But the jaguar."

"Selah. If we don't figure this out and get the information to the public, your father, and probably mother, will be murdered. If you prefer, we can carry Galon back and hand him over as well as ourselves. Do you want to do that?"

"Help me move him. This is too near that jaguar's snack. I understand what you're saying, but I won't be responsible for someone's death. We'll just have to come back for him before the ship leaves." I didn't wait for Reegan's answer but started dragging Galon over the fewest plants possible.

We found a dead tree with a large root system and curled him up in it. Then I climbed up the tree a little way and placed my mother's scarf on a branch so we would be able to find him again. I took one last sniff and then made my way down.

CHAPTER NINETEEN

We trekked far enough that we couldn't see the ship anymore. I spent a few moments in utter panic that I would get turned around until Reegan put a gentle hand on my arm.

"It's behind us. Keep it that way. We're only going a little farther," he said.

In yet another small clearing, this time with no sign of predators, he set his bag down and dug through it.

I put my bag down and unzipped it to retrieve some tools.

I saw the paperwork hiding there and tugged it out. I opened the first folder and found my birth certificate inside. Behind that was a stack of papers on my mother's pregnancy. I flipped through them.

Viable pregnancy

Possible twin

Questionable modification process

Signed off on

My eyes pulled the words from the text as if they were highlighted. Then I read as fast as I could.

Pregnancy will be allowed to move forward. Modification process was performed on one embryo on the second day as is standard, but there was a second undetected embryo. One twin has since perished and the tissue has been reabsorbed. There is no way of knowing which twin. Because of dwindling population we will not terminate the pregnancy. Fetus will be closely monitored and tested upon birth.

Dr. Beechwood signs off on a possibly non-modified pregnancy.

"Wait." I stopped reading. "What?"

Reegan read over my shoulder.

"That's not what I thought at all," he said.

"What does this mean?"

"Something completely different." He took a deep breath and held it. "It's possible you're not modified at all."

"How did this information not get out? They would have tested me at birth. How did I have a twin that wasn't modified?"

"Modification happens on day two, twins can form as late as day six. I did find some old research looking into how to check if someone was modified after birth. I'm talking extensive research. You would have thought reverse engineering the system would allow us to check for modification, but it doesn't. DNA is much too complicated for that. It's not easy to tell if you have the artificial genes or if you made them naturally. Maybe that's why you outgrew the seizures. Maybe your father thought that too."

My mind raced with the possibilities for what it could all mean. If I wasn't modified but had shown the signs of being so, the entire system would be broken. Modification would be obsolete. I had to get this information out. I glanced at the blue sky through the leaves above me. That ancient satellite better still be capable of sending files. I didn't know what was going to happen, but I knew we had to take a look at my DNA and get the info to my uncle.

Reegan bent back to his bag and then snuck up on a plant with a pair of tweezers as if it would run away. I held the sample jars out for him. At first his hand shook like the leaves he was trying to take. But he took a deep breath, squared his shoulders, and steadied his arm with his other hand. His stature was ridiculous, bent like an old man with a bad back, arms outstretched. A chill ran down my spine at the thought that all that stood between us and nature was this man-made material. I squeezed the jar I held, and my arm ached with the pressure I was putting on the glass. I did as Reegan had done and took a deep breath.

He grasped one leaf lightly with the tweezers and brought it smoothly over to the jar. He set it down inside so softly that I wasn't even sure he had given me anything. Then he reached for another, and another. I packaged them in separate jars and bags. One he put into a bag and then instructed me to pour a specific solution into the bag as well. Another he had me place in a jar and then sprinkled with some powder.

We finished gathering those leaves and then moved to another bush farther on. He took me to three locations in total and at the last one found some berries and nuts to add to the collection. It was then that I had a eureka moment.

"What if we collected some flesh from the jaguar's meal?" I held out yet another sample bag, the suit crackling as I shifted on my feet. The wind rustled the leaves. The smell of fresh plants was heady and intoxicating even through the filter in my hood.

"That's a really good idea," Reegan said without looking up from the pile of berries he squatted over.

Scenarios started running through my head. If the jaguar came back, could we fight it off? Probably not. If he was already there, could we bypass him without him caring? Probably not. So what was the best way to find if he had already returned or was anywhere nearby? I could definitely check if he was there before we came up to the clearing simply by climbing a tree. But would there be a dead one that I could climb? And would I be able to distinguish the jaguar from his natural camouflage? The entire situation sounded like a suicide mission, but wasn't that what we had been doing this entire time? Risking our lives? Pushing the limits to see if we could prove that the current system wasn't performing as it should be?

I decided to find a tree before we got close to the clearing and at least try to scout the area.

And we had to risk it. That flesh was much more likely to contain SE bacteria. Especially seeing as my father had run tests on plants before, and it turned out some didn't contain the SE bacteria at all.

Reegan started packing up. I ran my eyes over his body, checking and rechecking for gashes in the fabric or anything out of the ordinary. I was more frightened of him catching the SE bacteria than of the jaguar. He looked normal, although exhausted. I walked over to him and cupped his cheek in my hand.

"What was that for?" He smiled and put his hand over mine.

"We made it this far. I want to make sure you know how much I care about you before we possibly die at the jaws of a jaguar or get caught by Argana."

"Aw, thanks. I love you too, Selah." He pulled me into a hug, devoid of warmth due to the barrier between us, but comforting nonetheless.

When we let go, we heard the sound of voices, and it sent

us into a frenzy. Reegan finished placing jars and bags in his pack in a careful pattern, and we took off.

A hundred yards or so to the jaguar's clearing, I stopped Reegan at a giant, dead tree. I looked up its trunk, saddened by the fact that I couldn't name what type it was. The study of biology was based purely on hearsay for our generation. It was all book knowledge because there were no specimens to be utilized. I reached out to touch the tree. The bark was pitted and had deep grooves running through it. It was long dead, and probably unstable, but I figured it would get me high enough to see something. So I started my climb.

"I'll whistle if you need to come down," Reegan said.

I acknowledged him with a nod and then ascended. My muscles complained. It had been a long day already, and we still had to climb back up the ship. The bark crumbled under my fingertips in some places. In others I would find a foothold by kicking through. The worst was when I reached for the next spot and the tree groaned. I hadn't climbed anything so volatile before. Rock was predictable. Metal was obvious.

I did reach a good height though and was able to see the tree where we had left Galon and my scarf blowing in the wind. I was also able to see just to the side of that, where the jaguar had been. The carcass was still there, but the jaguar wasn't. From what I could see of the surrounding area, he wasn't anywhere around. But I was still uncertain because of his hiding ability. We would just have to take that risk.

I climbed back down to Reegan and dusted my hands on my pants.

"That was a little bit terrifying," I said.

"And the ship wasn't?"

"The ship was easy."

I laughed at the shock on his face. We went slowly back to the tree where Galon lay. He was curled in a ball and still breathing. We went beyond him to the clearing and stepped out toward the carcass. Nothing jumped on us. Reegan gathered a few samples of meat, all while holding our breath and trying not to really look at the mangled body and bones of some poor creature. The veins running through the flesh were still intact, and the muscle was built of tiny strings still attached to the bone with sinew. It was fascinating. And disgusting. Especially when bile spilled from the slice Reegan opened with a scalpel.

It all felt so easy. I released the tension in my calves and shoulders. A twig snapped, and all that intensity returned, my body tuned like a taught rope. But nothing came, and we were able to pack up again. We made it back to the edge of the jungle and the ship. The ground was crawling with WHO agents and even scientists and a few modified all decked out and astronaut-like on our home world. Apparently the plank could angle to the ground.

"Do you think we could just walk back up?" Reegan asked.

"I doubt it. Our suits don't hide our faces that well."

"Then what do we do?"

"The only way to get back into the ship and have time to look at the samples in the lab is if we go up the other side. We can get to the access hatch from there."

We hadn't thought about it before, but the ship having stopped farther into the jungle was a good thing now. We could sneak around the ship without being seen. By the time we reached the bow, or helm—we weren't quite sure which was which on the symmetrical oblong shape—we were standing on sand and free of the people marching around. We could finally discontinue the exhausting work of slinking through trees without touching anything. We both stood tall and reached our arms to the sky, stretching luxuriously.

"The best spot to climb is actually on the far side of the bow," I said. "The bow itself is too slippery because it's built to plow the air, but next to it on either side are joists we can climb."

"Why not this side so we don't have as far to walk?" Reegan's voice shook a bit as he craned his head back to see the height of the ship.

"I'm worried we'll be seen."

"We'll be seen as soon as we reach the observation deck."

"Yes. But until then we can avoid it. The ledge is sufficiently big, trust me."

"You've walked it?" His voice squeaked with indignation.

"I've seen it, and I'm very good at judging the size of things from a distance." I slapped him on the back and walked out into the sand. It was exhausting in its own way, and we were both panting by the time we reached the joist at the base of the ship.

Reegan again bent backward to look up, and color drained from his face when he realized we would almost be hanging horizontally at one point. The angle from the base of the ship was drastic. Coming down, he hadn't seen it, plus we had used the tree.

I swung my bag over both shoulders and then took his backpack from him.

"We're gonna do it the same way. You follow me up. Pay attention to my hands and feet. And don't look down. Got it?"

He nodded and gulped.

I hopped up to the first handhold, swung my legs around, and prepared for the adrenaline rush to hit me. I so hoped my body had enough left. This wasn't going to be easy, and this wasn't the end.

Reegan followed slowly. I checked on him every few reaches, but I had to be careful I didn't look beyond him to the ground below and risk vertigo. I loved climbing like I loved breathing, but I was still human and certainly still capable of fear.

When we reached the apex of the curve, I hung from my fingertips for just a moment before pulling myself over and up. The weight of gravity sent a thrill through me. I wanted to hang there even longer, but I didn't want Reegan to notice. I allowed myself that one moment of bliss and then continued on. Reegan grunted and groaned behind me, and I watched him from the safety of a small ledge as he swung up the curve. His shoulders were shaking. I wondered how much physical training he had been doing so far this year. He had been holed up in a science lab too long.

He reached the ledge and held on with his entire arm so he could rest. Above the curve, we lost the protection of the ship. The shade was gone. The sun beat down on us without mercy. The wind brought some relief, until a gust blew sand around us like an angry tornado. I looked up to the ledge we were aiming for and wanted to cry. It was so far away.

"We can do it," Reegan breathed.

"Ok."

The first thing I really felt was the bags weighing me down.

The next thing was the sun burning my neck with an intensity I wasn't used to. The suit provided a UV block, but I was rarely outside this long and the heat was relentless.

Then I received a gift from the wind—a blast of sand. Behind it came a hot, strong gust which nearly dislodged my fingers. I clung on with only the first knuckles of my right hand and my left toes. This time it wasn't a free hang for pleasure. I swung back and grabbed with my left hand. I nearly hugged the ship, but the metal was hot, so I avoided pressing my cheek against it.

The metal started searing through my suit, and I climbed ever faster to be able to move my hands as quickly as possible. I barely had a chance to look back and check on Reegan, and when I reached another small ledge and paused, I saw that he was farther behind than he should have been. I feared calling out to him would attract attention, so I watched and waited.

His speed was slow but steady. He finally came up beside me and sat on the tiny bar next to me.

"It's hot," he wheezed.

"Not much farther," I said.

"I don't know if I can do it." He held his palms out. The gloves were wet through, making the climb slick as ice. I took a rag from the bag and ripped it in half. Then I bandaged his palms over the gloves, leaving his fingers free and barely adding any thickness. It was a small dry surface, but hopefully it would be enough.

"You can. You have to."

I kissed him on the cheek through our suits and then turned to keep climbing. When I looked back after three moves, he was coming up behind me.

The next difficult part lay ahead—the glass of the observation deck. Because we were close to a joist, I wasn't too worried about being seen, but the glass was even more slick and hot than the metal. Shimmying up the joist while lying on baked glass was not comfortable. It seemed everyone inside was either facing the other direction or had gone outside, so even though we had cover, we didn't have a worry at all. The sun was far enough overhead that our shadows were cast down instead of into the room. We would go undetected.

The ledge finally shaded my vision, just barely. I had to pull my arm farther back than I had so far to grip the edge. And it had a lovely lip which made the pull even easier. I hung from it for a second before swinging my legs over, and then I stood and faced into the wind. I leaned into the force, on top of the world.

Reegan pulled up next to me, and I took in the unfettered beauty of sand as far as I could see. There was no glass between me and the view this time. The blue sky above me was more round than I remembered from last being outside. The clouds were fluffier than they looked from inside the holo-studio, with more color and texture as they danced about.

"Let's get this over with," Reegan grumbled. His breathing was even again, but the fatigue on his face was evident. He wasn't going to last much longer on this hell-bent chase.

He stood and walked away from me, around the bow. When we came near the other side, and started catching glimpses of people among the foliage below, we went to hands and knees, and then to bellies. The metal was searing.

The access hatch was beyond the main door. Above the plank, I peeked over and saw no one, but I had no visual of the entranceway. Reegan scooted himself around until we faced each other. His head was on his crossed arms like we were just sunbathing and having a chat.

"We have to stand up to get the hatch open."

"Where does it lead?"

"Unfortunately, because of the need for decontamination, right into a side chamber that then goes into the main entrance vault."

I took a deep breath.

"I say we just go for it."

"What if we're outnumbered?"

"Not possible. From who I can see below, most of the people we have to worry about are down there. Otherwise it'll be the younger generation and a few of your generation. But what do they care about us? Even if they know we're the problem."

"Good point." I surveyed the people below. "Where's Argana?"

"She's one I haven't seen. She could be in the jungle."

"I doubt she would dirty her precious heels in that mess. I don't think that woman has any love for nature."

"We can take Argana."

"In the state we're in?" We had been on the run for nearly eight hours, climbed the ship down, survived the jungle as far as we could tell, been in a fight with Galon, and climbed *back* up.

"If we hadn't eaten for three weeks and been running for two days, we could take Argana. I've never been scared of her physical abilities. I'm terrified what she might do when her henchmen catch up with us, but I only fear her mind."

We wiggled our way past the plank and over to the hatch. Reegan took a moment to figure out the mechanism.

"This lever has to be pulled and then this wheel turned completely three times. The seal should release and then it won't take much effort to pull it up."

He grabbed my hand and kissed it. Then we got up into squats. I glanced behind to see if we were visible, and of course if anyone looked up we were on full display.

"When the seal releases, I'll count to three and we'll stand and jump in as quickly as possible."

The lever slid easily, the wheel not so much. But together we managed to turn it three times. Then nothing happened.

"So, now what?" I said.

Another moment passed. Reegan stood and kicked the hatch. It released a strong hiss. He started hauling on the wheel, and I stood to help. Another heave and we had it open. We leaped into the dark below without waiting to find out if we had been seen.

We landed in a small decontamination chamber. The sprayers sputtered to life and fogged our view. When they finished, we both unzipped our hoods and stripped our suits off.

"I feel like I can breathe again," I whispered.

Then the door to the entrance vault opened automatically.

Argana stood there with one hip cocked and her arms crossed. Her eyes bugged out wide when we appeared.

"Hello," Reegan said. "Funny to see you here. Aren't you terrified you'll breathe some bacteria?"

"We both know that's not possible. Yet." Her silence held so much weight. I almost thought she meant it as a threat, as if she planned to make it so herself. As if the SE bacteria were under her control. "You think you know everything. I love that. Keep up that confidence, Reegan. You'll need it."

"When you take me to the courts?"

"When I take you. Period." She stepped forward slightly, the threat pushing ahead of her like a strong wind.

"You have no power over us." The steadiness of his voice surprised me, especially since he had admitted his fear of her control.

"You don't quite understand what I have power over. This world is mine for the taking, and you right along with it." She spread her arms wide, as if to envelop and swallow the jungle whole.

I shivered.

It was that moment the decontamination sprayers chose to turn on again. We were instantly shielded in a haze, and I yanked Reegan to the wall to run past Argana. But as we started sprinting through the observation deck to the stairs, she called to the people on the ground, and we kicked it up a notch.

CHAPTER TWENTY

My thoughts bounced around in my head as we ran. I couldn't quite get a handle on what felt wrong about what Argana had said. Was she just crazy? Was I crazy? Or had I really heard the things I thought I had heard? How much power did she really have?

The questions just kept pinging around until we reached the science level and Reegan pulled me into my father's lab, still a complete mess. He locked the door behind us and set straight to work pulling out the sample jars and prepping equipment. I hooked his tablet up to the lock so no one else could get in and righted some of the tables and helped him where I could. Then I sat in a chair while he took a sample of my blood and sent it through the right machines to be able to parse out and view the DNA strands.

He then put on another suit and stepped into the small fume hood chamber in the corner of the office. I watched through the glass, my fingers pressed up like a child staring through a window. He opened a jar with some of the meat, and the smell made him retch. He put it directly into the first machine and chose a leaf as his second sample, leaving the rest of the flesh to be opened later if we needed it. He sent a berry through the process as well.

I went out to the hallway to check if the coast was clear. So far no one had come after us, but I knew it was only a matter of time. Then I heard footsteps, but I could swear they were coming up the stairs, not down. I waited by the door.

But the face I saw turn the corner was a friendly one. It was Jimman and the other maintenance workers. I opened the door a sliver.

"How can we help?" Jimman said with a wide smile.

"Shouldn't you be fixing the ship?"

"Some of my men are. The rest of us are here."

I hesitated but Reegan came up behind and swung the door wide. He welcomed them into the room and then locked the door behind them. "Argana knows we're in here. We just need time."

"That we can give you. Not a problem."

"You don't have to do this, you know."

The maintenance workers around him filled the room with their bulk. Some ogled the machines. Others watched my face with awe. I wondered what I looked like after the day we'd been through.

"We've got your back. No worries."

Then he did something I didn't expect at all—he hugged me. I didn't want to let go. When I did, he turned to Reegan and shook hands.

They marched out with purpose, ready to make a stand.

"Have you found anything?" I asked Reegan while I locked the door and pulled a table in front of it.

"Come look."

He pulled out the chair for me. In the microscope I saw two separate DNA strands, curled and twisted, ladder-like, colorful.

"Yours is on the right. The berry is on the left. It did contain SE, a very strong set."

"What am I looking for?"

"They're similar. You see recurring patterns. Right?"

I picked my head up from the microscope. I needed to see his face as I asked.

"Am I modified? Does this mean I'm sick?"

"No. It means you're evolving."

It wasn't until that sentence came out of his mouth, this late in my life, that I realized one's heart could actually stop for a millisecond and then begin beating again. The idea had never crossed my mind, but now that he said it, all the pieces fell into place, and the last few months made sense. Why had I never seen this option?

He pointed to the microscope again, and I dropped my face to the glass.

"See the purple strand I'm focusing on? That's the same on both." He put commands into the computer, and the microscope zoomed to another area. "And those green stripes on that strand? Those are also the same."

"But what do they do?"

"They're the building blocks of certain systems. My strands are not that color at all. In fact, on a normal human, those strands may not exist, or they're in the process of dying."

A shout sounded outside the door, jerking us out of our bubble of discovery.

"Here, look at this." He pulled me over to a screen with lines of code. "This is your genetic code. I ran it through the computer just now, of course I can't parse all of it, but I searched specifically for the mutation that we force into every modified, the control that causes us to seize. Yours is here," he pointed his finger.

"So it's there."

"It exists. But it's not the same as mine."

He typed a few things into the computer, and a similar screen came up parallel. A loud bang came from the hallway, and we both jumped. Reegan's hand shook now as he adjusted his gene code to the same spot as mine. He lined up the lines. There was a very similar looking line on his code, except for a few letters that didn't quite match.

"What does this mean?"

"Your genetics added a code similar to the one we created for the control. We created it not just to test. We created it to protect the modified from the seizures normal humans are having. You made yours simply by evolving."

"But why did I react to the stimulant all these years?"

"I assume because your body had protected you against seizures but hadn't yet figured out how to protect you from our stimulants. You were never modified, Selah. You were born with these natural protections. Your skin is darker than mine because you're evolving naturally." He compared our skin.

Something, or someone, crashed into the door. Through the window we could see the maintenance workers defending themselves against the WHO bodyguards.

Reegan picked up my uncle's device, already plugged into the system and downloading this whole time. He started typing a message.

"It's not going very quickly," he said. "Just like your uncle warned us."

I glanced at the screen and cringed at the loading bar that crept along steadily.

"He's not even sure if those satellites are functioning properly. What if the information gets lost?"

A hand smacked the window behind us. I flinched.

I barricaded the door with more chairs and tables. Then I stopped.

"Reegan. We have nowhere to go."

"No, we don't."

"We have to give ourselves up. We'll leave the device here and give it time to send. It's the only chance." He put Rusty in a cabinet and turned the key.

"What if it doesn't finish sending? We'll never know," I said.

"We'll pretend like we do know. Argana only needs to fear the possibility."

A cold chill worked its way down my spine. What if the information didn't get out, and Argana killed us? We were the only ones who knew.

We stared into each other's eyes. Then he nodded and helped me move the tables and chairs away from the door. He ran out into the hallway and shouted at everyone to stop. I watched, mesmerized, through the window as things played out. In slow motion the fight came to an end, a few more punches finding their mark here or there, but it petered out soon enough.

"Take us to Argana." Reegan waved for me to come out with him.

And we marched with the henchmen to our doom.

CHAPTER TWENTY-ONE

They marched us upstairs. I had expected to descend, so I peeked back at Reegan to see if he had thought the same. He raised his eyebrows at me and shrugged his shoulders.

They didn't put any restraints on us, but we were both flanked and pushed at a pace our bodies weren't capable of. I had never felt such exhaustion in my life.

We ended up on the top floor, above the observation deck, up a staircase I hadn't even realized existed. But of course it should have, because where else would Argana have her lair but on top of the ship—and completely made of glass so she had an amazing vantage point at all times. Just like the holo-studio and the observation deck, I could see metal shielding tucked away outside the glass to protect it from the sand storms. It was also a special, purple-tinted UV glass that protected her white skin while allowing her the freedom of being in sunlight. I only now realized she didn't have a service dog. Was that the job of her henchmen who never left her side?

The room was large and consisted of a living area and

sleeping area as well as an overpowering desk. She sat at said desk, presiding over her dominion, as we walked in and were told to kneel in front of her. Neither of us did. This wasn't a kingdom. There would be no kneeling. When we didn't listen, a door to Argana's left opened. It was an elevator, which seemed like a huge waste of power.

Out stepped Galon. And my father.

Galon pushed him forward. I ran to him as he fell to the ground. His clothing was dirty, his hair was a mess, and he looked skinnier than usual, which was really saying something. I captured him and held him on my lap, tears beginning to leak from my eyes.

"Selah." He dropped his head to my shoulder, the weight pressing down on both of us.

"Father. What happened?"

"I presume you'll find out now."

Galon strode forward and kicked me away from my father. The hate in his eyes had gone to an entirely new level. If I had thought the man I once knew was no longer inside Galon, now there wasn't a man at all. Other than a few scratches and bruises from the jungle, he seemed fine.

"You look healthy," I said to Galon. "I just hope you didn't touch any SE while we were out there." Then I pushed myself to standing and helped my father up. I took his arm in mine, and we went to stand in front of Argana.

"Welcome," she said. "I'm happy to have you here."

"Of course you are," Reegan grumbled.

She simply nodded and smiled. This was going to be fun for her.

"What do you want?" I asked.

"Your father here has been in our custody because he is a danger to the public."

"Custody? You mean imprisoned. And the only danger to the public here is you. What are you hiding from us?" I said.

Out of the corner of my eye I saw Reegan perk up. Apparently he hadn't caught on to the same things I had, and we hadn't really had time to discuss it around finding out I was evolving. Now was my chance to see if my theories were true. If I thought my world had been blown to bits with everything already, I was in for a real awakening if my entire world was a lie and the WHO had caused the downfall of our species. I wasn't sure I could put the pieces back together again this time. But I had to know.

"The question is: what is your father hiding from us? Dr. Beechwood here is closed mouthed. He's very good at keeping secrets. Of course that's part of why we hired him in the first place, when the first round of modifications went horribly wrong, but it's come back to bite us. All this time I've been working away at him, but he just won't budge. Perhaps if his precious daughter feels a bit of the pain, he'll speak? Your father has to answer for his mistakes."

Before I had a chance to open my mouth or make a move, Galon was on top of my father, wrestling him away from me. Galon used one arm to launch me a few feet away. It knocked the wind out of me. While I regained my composure, Galon was shoving my father into a chair and buckling restraints around him. Reegan lunged forward but was caught short by another man.

"Thank you, Galon. You can hook up the machines now."

He took nodes and started attaching them to my father's body. My father just sat there, not fighting back. What had they been doing to him? I wrenched free of my captor's arms toward the chair, and my fingers fumbled with the first restraint. Galon shoved me away again, and I lunged back. The henchmen stepped in and bound my wrists. They plunked us down in our own chairs but didn't tie us down.

"What are you going to do to him?" I asked through the sobs.

Argana stood up, placing her hands on the table and tapping her fingers slowly. Then she sighed. "Selah, I need you to understand what the problem is. Your father knows things that he can't share with the general public. So far he hasn't shared those things, but he also has a secret that he *needs* to share... with me. I believe it has something to do with you."

I avoided glancing at Reegan. I couldn't risk Argana realizing we knew that secret too. "He's spent his time with us *not* sharing the information. He is incredibly willful. It has come to this."

"Why didn't you just kill him?" Reegan said.

"What would be the fun in that?"

My jaw dropped open, and Argana laughed.

"I'm only joking. Why would I kill one of the brightest minds in the world? We have no room to be disposing of people on a whim. Dr. Beechwood still has a use for the WHO and the modification project. But for now I need him to tell me the missing piece to the puzzle."

She dragged a finger along my cheek as she circled me. I jumped away from the touch.

"And then there's this little issue of you sending the ship into the jungle and performing some interesting feats. We're not quite sure why you did what you did, so we must assume it has to do with the same secret."

Well crap. Now I glanced at Reegan.

He winked at me.

"Don't worry. Punishment for your actions will come in due time." She pinched my ear. "For now, I need to know the information. I need to be able to assess the risks and take into account what will happen to you and your father and Reegan here, but also how this will affect society. There are so many people involved, and you three seem to be forgetting that I'm here to protect our species."

I barked out a short laugh.

"I know your feelings on the subject. I don't need the commentary, thank you." She clenched her teeth and combed a hand through my hair. "I'm in control of what happens to our tiny world. We're losing the battle against nature, and we need a leg up. I believe this secret your father is keeping is what we require."

During that last sentence, I glanced over at her brother. He flinched when she mentioned nature. I wondered why she believed he wouldn't act on his true self. He didn't believe in all this crap about fixing the human race. What would he think of me?

"Does the UN know what you're doing here?" Reegan asked.

"The UN knows that for the greater good they need to keep their noses out of specific business."

"That's a comfort. I thought for a second there that they were condoning torture."

"Oh the torture they certainly condone." The wicked smile that crossed her face was one I never wanted to see again. She picked up a remote from her desk and fingered it fondly, then handed it to Galon.

"So if they know about the torture, what *are* you keeping from them?" I asked.

"I can't disclose that information. But it's something much worse than you're imagining."

I knew with that comment that we had her hooked. She wanted to tell us. She longed to reveal and show off. We would get it out of her—it was just a matter of finessing the language so she felt she had all the power.

"I'm terrified," Reegan said in monotone.

She pointed to Father, and Galon tapped a button on the remote. Father went into convulsions for a second, and then Galon tapped the button again. Father sat still, panting and drooling a little. I jumped up from my chair but felt so help-less with my hands tied that I stayed where I was.

"Dr. Beechwood, let's get on with things. I would like to know what it is that you discovered. What are you keeping from me?" Argana went to him and bent down to look him in the face. She even went as far as to wipe his drool with a cloth.

"Selah, don't listen to her," he said.

Argana reached out and touched the button herself. Father shook in the chair until she tapped it again.

"This isn't fun," she said. "I would much rather we sit down for tea and talk things out. You know I don't enjoy hurting you, Reuel. And I especially don't want to hurt Selah," she paused, "Or Abira."

Father jumped against the buckles and straps at the sound of my mother's name in Argana's mouth.

She ambled over to me and petted my hair again, suddenly grabbing a handful and forcing my head back. Her fingers danced over my face from chin to forehead.

"Sit down," she said.

I didn't.

Her other hand punched me in the kidney and I crumpled into the chair.

"Thank you," she said. A blindfold fell over my eyes, and I felt my ankles fastened to the chair legs. Someone lifted my arms behind me, taking no care to make it easy—my shoulders screamed but I kept my mouth shut—and draped them over the back of the chair. I was stuck fast. My breathing increased.

The quiet blanketed me like the darkness. It seemed everyone had left. Then I felt it, cold metal tracing patterns on my bare arm. Someone took hold of my finger. After that I came to and heard the screaming, my screaming. The pain in my finger ripped the cries from my throat without my consent.

"Stop, stop!" my father yelled. Reegan's voice and Galon's both filtered through the fog of pain, raised and angry but incomprehensible.

The pain lessened but it still ached and burned up my arm.

Then I felt the touch of the metal again. It tickled my cheek gently. Then it sliced the sensitive skin there. I gasped.

It sliced my forearm.

It sliced my calf.

A hand took hold of my foot and the boot was removed. I fought the ties that held me. The chair squeaked against the floor. My sock was removed. The metal nicked the top of my foot. A hand took hold of my toe. I whimpered.

"I'll tell you. Stop."

"No," I whispered. If Argana knew, she would have no reason to keep us alive. But the hand left my toe and the blindfold was pulled down. Argana used the cloth to blot at the blood running form the cut on my cheek.

"But it won't do you any good. You can't stop a rolling boulder. It will roll right over you and keep on going," Father said.

"I have great power. Believe me. I can stop whatever it is you've set in motion."

Father laughed and kept laughing. Argana pulled back.

"I did nothing," he said. "Your cruel nature did the work for me."

"Let me put things straight," she said. "I didn't create this world. I merely tried to fix it and failed miserably. I didn't make us stop evolving. Nature did that all on her own. I only tried to help her get restarted by creating *Staphylococcus evolutio*."

And there it was.

Reegan's mouth dropped open.

I laughed. My finger still throbbed, but I laughed. She would lose. There was nothing she could do to stop nature. Galon had been right all along.

Argana whipped around to face me.

"What's so funny?" she said.

"Nature is fighting back." I gazed into Father's eyes. My father. More a part of me than I had ever thought. And he looked back with love and admiration... and a tiny smirk.

"Selah is evolving," Father said.

"Good, but what did you do? How did you make her do that?" Argana ran up to him and shook him by his shoulders.

The chair legs rattled on the floor. Galon stood behind Father, his face turning a lovely shade of puce.

"Selah isn't modified," Reegan said.

Argana stopped shaking my father and stood slowly. Then she turned on her heel and walked over to Reegan. She hauled him to his feet and looked him in the eye.

"What did you just say?"

"Reegan, stop!" My eyes were locked on Galon, who held a knife to my father's throat.

"No, please, continue. I'd like to hear what you have to say." Galon's eyebrows rose.

Father swallowed, and the movement caused the knife to nick him. A trickle of blood spilled down his neck.

"Selah isn't modified." Reegan spoke slowly, letting the words sink in to the heaviness of the room. "She never was. She had a twin who was modified, but that twin died, and the scientists couldn't tell which one was modified. I have the DNA strains to prove it."

"Where are they?" Argana screamed.

"Shut up, Argana," Galon said.

She clamped her mouth shut and looked at him, her cheeks pale as the sun-drenched sky. "Just shut up. Your insane babbling is giving me a headache."

"Galon, please," she said. "This information can't get out. If people know the modified project isn't working, we'll have investigations. We need to fix the evolving problem so we can then battle the SE."

"It's your own fault. You created the bacteria, so you can deal with that. I've added it to your list of sins. I always knew you were pretty stupid. Yet you never listened. You never heard. All you could think of was your own life."

"It was in the name of science." Argana seemed to be composing herself again, gaining height with a straighter posture and a stronger voice. "We would have been wiped out anyway in time."

"Oh, I'm sure of that," Galon said. "And you, my dear sister, will be the first to go. You deserve a little dose of your own medicine. I always told you not to mess with the natural order of things. Now I'll let your manufactured order be your punishment."

One of the henchmen, Darm I thought, was circling behind Galon, but he wasn't good at sneaking, and Galon whipped around to face him.

"You try anything, and you'll get the knife first." When he pointed the tip of his knife at the man, Reegan lunged forward to knock Galon over. Galon swung the knife around and sliced Reegan's cheek.

Reegan fell back, blood gushing down his neck, his arms awkwardly pinned beneath his weight. Galon's arm was still around my father, and his balance was off. He stumbled back, dragging the chair across the floor, emitting a giant screech. He regained his feet and put the knife back to my father's jugular.

"Galon," my father whispered.

"Yes?"

"It doesn't have to happen this way. We can work together to make sure nature takes its course."

"You don't really understand. Nature has already taken its course. It just needs my help to rid the world of people like you and Argana."

"I now agree with you," Father said. "We shouldn't be meddling with the natural order. Selah is proof of that."

Galon pulled the knife a little tighter to my father's skin and cut off his talking.

"Perhaps Selah is meant to be, but she might be a one-off. We'll have to wait and see if it happens again on its own." He turned to me, and his hatred hit me like a blaze of fire. "Selah is also a little bitch who deserves to die just for the havoc she's wreaked."

"Galon, this is pointless," Argana said. "No one need die."

"Really? Wasn't that your plan all along? After torturing the information out of them, you were going to kill all three of them. I mean, they know your secret, and there's no guarantee that they'll keep it."

Argana's face blanched even whiter than I thought possible. Apparently she had been so lost in the moment that she hadn't realized how much she had revealed. It was time for me to step in.

"Even if Argana intended to kill us, this isn't who you are, Galon. I know you. And this isn't you. You might believe what the radicals say, that nature should be allowed to rule, but is a human killing a human what nature wants? I'm a natural human like you, but I'm evolving. I'm natural."

"You don't know me. You haven't known me since you created that horrible hologram. The evil that lives inside you will never be balanced out by the fact that you're evolving. And Argana, death and destruction is nature's course. You should let it go. Let it happen. People like Dr. Beechwood need to be removed from the equation."

And then he ran the knife across my father's throat. Blood poured out. My father choked.

I watched from afar, tied to a chair, as my father bled. Reegan wiggled toward him. I threw my chair to the floor, and my hands broke free. With no care for the chair still tied to my legs, I crawled to my father and knelt down to put my forehead to my father's.

"I love you," I whispered. "I'm sorry. I don't know what to do. What do I do?"

Reegan was beside me then. He contorted himself out of his binds and ripped them off with his teeth. Then he yanked mine apart. I pulled my father into my lap. He gazed up at me, choking on his own blood. I was bathed in it.

Then it was over. His breathing halted, his eyes glassed over, and it was done. My father was dead. In my arms.

I screamed.

CHAPTER TWENTY-TWO

Darm barreled into Galon. Trej also jumped forward with a third man running from the door. All three had him tackled to the ground within seconds. They dragged him back into the elevator.

"This is what is meant to be!" His fingers scrabbled for purchase on the floor, but they found no help. "The world will fall. Nature will win out. You will have to let it happen. You will have no choice!"

The door shut, cutting off his voice.

I still sat on the floor, my hands splayed to either side of me and a puddle of blood circling my father and me. The tears didn't stop, though they were silent. My father was gone. Completely and absolutely gone. I had just gotten him back, and now I would never have him again.

More guards came in the room and went for my father's body. I screamed and latched onto him.

"Get away from him!" I cried. It came through my vocal chords with a guttural growl that burned sharply.

"Selah, please." Reegan squeezed my shoulder.

I violently shrugged away and dropped my head over my father, cocooning him with my body. I shut it all out—the iron tang of my father's blood, the skin that felt like putty now, Reegan's voice as he attempted to sooth me, Argana's voice as she gave orders, the sun shining through the glass and warming us, the fact that my father was dead.

I was holding a dead body.

I held a corpse.

The thought sickened me so much that I vomited. Reegan took the opportunity to grab me and haul me back, away from my father.

The guards jumped forward and pulled my father away from the room. They dragged his body along the floor, but he didn't fight back like Galon had. His body was limp and bent at a strange angle. His blood left a sickening path.

"Selah?" Reegan whispered at my shoulder. "Let's get you cleaned up."

Reegan brought a cool cloth to my face. I sank into his arms, and we both tumbled to the floor. Tears streamed down his face, agony painted across his features. He could barely meet my eyes.

"And that is why we should control the population even more," Argana said.

I would have leapt at her, strangled her with my bare hands, if it hadn't been for my utter exhaustion and inability to move my limbs.

"The radicals are a danger, not only to my operations but to the public. I'll have it looked into—"

"He's your brother!" I interrupted.

"A brother who stood in the way of what needs to be done. Though I do have to say that Galon is correct in one thing. You two will need to be taken care of."

"You mean disposed of." Reegan's arms tightened around me.

"However you wish to phrase it."

"You might not want to do that," I croaked.

"I didn't hear you. Can you repeat yourself please?" Argana leaned toward me but not close enough to be touched. She sneered at the smell.

"My uncle knows that I'm not modified."

"And how would he know that?"

"Because we sent him a message before we gave ourselves up to your henchmen." I pushed away from Reegan and pushed away from the floor, forcing my body to a standing position. My clothes dripped blood, and my heart beat with the effort of staying vertical and sane, but I needed to face her head on.

"You can't have. The system has been down. Plus I blocked your account."

"Oh, Argana. I wish you understood how little you know about the people you supposedly control. They have no love for your system. You think the radicals are the only ones who don't trust the UN? You think in a population this size that you can control them all? You think they are all sheep? You are sadly mistaken. I have had contact with my uncle through a device of his own making. He's an engineer. I believe you know that." I paused, letting the idea sink in and watching her pupils dilate and her wrinkles deepen.

Reegan stood and came up behind me. The warmth of his solid body at my back was a buffer against the cold creeping into my bones. I still had Reegan and Mother and Uncle Tobias. I was in no way alone. And no matter what happened, I was one hundred percent a product of my parents. I was not a science experiment. I was real.

"So the world will know." Argana sucked in a tight breath and put two fingers to her mouth.

"And we will tell them about SE," Reegan said. "You're finished. So if you feel like killing us, go for it, but you'll pay for that as well as your other mistakes. We'll take over from here. A UN ship will be on its way soon because of the alarms from the ship hitting the jungle. I'll let them know what's happened. Feel free to take a seat, or maybe you need to lie down? You look a little pale."

Argana fell back onto her backside as if a chair had been at the ready for her.

Reegan brought me a chair and went to the control console at her desk.

"You won't get away with this." Argana still sat on the cold metal floor on the other side of the room, not having moved from where she fell.

"I don't want to talk to you, Argana. It's a waste of my breath," I said.

The sun began to set. Orange painted the sky outside the windows, and a tiny silhouette of a ship appeared on the far horizon.

Argana stood and went to the glass. Then she whipped around and strode over to me, towering above me. "You won't get away with it!"

As her hands reached down to grasp me, mine reached up to meet them. I gripped her wrists and squeezed. Then I used the leverage to stand and push her back. She squeaked as I shoved her backward. We went quickly, so quickly that she stumbled and lost one of her heels. Then she hit the glass, the beautiful orange and pink sky behind her.

"I said I don't want to talk."

I dropped her wrists with incredible force and walked away, straight into Reegan's arms. The tears began to flow again. I would never be able to stop them.

CHAPTER TWENTY-THREE

Reegan went to the holopanel in the observation deck. This was the one place on the ship where one could broadcast to the rest of the ship, and he did just that. He explained to the people standing in the glass dome, the people in the cafeteria, the people in the maintenance levels, the people in the holo-studio, the people in their bunks. He told them everything.

And when he was finished, the UN ship, which had been growing larger behind him as he spoke, landed on the sand not far from us. Soldiers poured out and found their way to the lowered plank. They came aboard, as did a general, and when they asked where Argana was, everyone pointed to Reegan.

At first they misunderstood and went to take him into custody. This caused an uproar from those assembled. In shock, the soldiers stopped and listened as the people told them what had happened. This was how we would expose Argana. It had nothing to do with my uncle knowing the truth. It had nothing to do with a special messaging system. It had everything to do with a people that knew what they needed to survive in this world and a people that would stand up for themselves. Secrets and diversions were not necessary when the population sought survival. We would survive together or not at all. And so, together we would expose Argana and the WHO for what they had done.

Reegan took the soldiers upstairs, and they took Argana into custody. When they brought her back down, the crowd didn't cheer or boo.

Silence reigned, and that was right.

The UN restarted our communications system and allowed me one live call back to the city. The hologram of my mother appeared before me, and I folded into a heap. She fell to her knees and reached out for me, feeling only pixels on her end.

"Selah?"

"I'm sorry, Mother. So sorry. I failed." Sobs punched their way through my throat.

Tears ran down her face while her hand caressed my hair. I couldn't feel it, but when I took her hand in mine we both felt a semblance of comfort in the cold solidity of the hologram.

"He's gone," she said.

"He wasn't," I choked out and another groan burst from my chest. "He was here the whole time, being tortured for information. He was here."

"You did what you could," she said.

"I didn't!" I screamed.

"Oh my child," she said. "You did. This wasn't your fault. You did not fail. Your father knows that. I know that. You could never fail us. Now come home to me so I can hold you."

The hologram cut out.

"What happened?" I scrambled to hold onto the pixels as they dissolved. "Bring her back! What happened!"

A UN soldier came to my side. "The satellites aren't perfect. We won't know when we'll have contact again. I'll come and get you if we do." He helped me to my feet and from the room. I found Reegan and asked him to put me to work compiling data.

Over the next few days, the engineers from the UN fixed what needed fixing on the ship. It was serviceable, and Jimman was able to work wonders since he knew the ship like a lover. He and his maintenance crew had only cuts and bruises and a few broken bones. They had survived their part of the fight.

While they did that, Reegan and I compiled the information from my DNA and the samples. We collected even more samples, and during our forays into the jungle, we realized the animals there weren't any more aggressive than expected. In fact, they seemed terrified of us. It wasn't what we had been told. Docile animals had turned rabid and vengeful for no apparent reason, or so they had said.

That led us to Argana's personal computers, and we found that the scientists who had been massacred by dolphins and pandas had been testing *Staphylococcus evolutio*. The bacteria didn't actually like animals. It preferred humans. When forced upon animal species it had turned them basically rabid.

When Reegan found that little tidbit, he busted out laughing.

"What?" My eyes were red and sore from reading and crying. I rubbed them.

"I can fix that."

"You can?"

"All of the research we've done with the modification leaned toward making us more like animals. We thought that since the animals were evolving, maybe we needed to step backward and become animal again. But with your DNA, we should be able to figure out how to meld the two. If we're more like animals, the bacteria should eventually stop attacking us."

"That's incredible."

"You could save us all."

"Stop. Don't do that please. In fact, would it be possible to stay anonymous somehow?"

"I think it might be too late for that. But we'll protect you." His hand landed on mine.

I looked up into his eyes and dove into the warmth there. I wanted to escape. I leaned forward and kissed him gently. Then I pulled back. "Nope."

He laughed and went back to work.

We did find Borno. Argana's elevator led to the dungeons she had built into the ship. There was no other access, and Borno had been stuck in a cell by himself. When we came in the door, he lay in a heap in the corner closest to the engines where it was warmest.

I ran to him. His ribcage lifted and sank with each breath, barely. His silky coat was now matted and dirty and brittle.

"My darling boy."

The sight of him made me cry. The fact that he would never see my father again made me howl in pain. Reegan brought water and sponged it into Borno's mouth. He started to perk up enough that we could carry him to the elevator. In Argana's room, we lay him on the bed and fed him mush for days. He gained strength with each meal.

By the time the ship was ready to leave, Borno was walking again. I hoped the sight of his sister and my mother would have him jumping again, but I worried that he knew my father was gone. Even with his strength regained, he still wasn't his old self.

Jimman came to give us a rundown on the situation. He didn't stay long though, as there was much to be done. And we were soon on our way back to the harbor, and then in the buses on the way to the city.

The trip home was more dangerous than usual. We were traveling in high summer. The burn teams hadn't gone ahead of us, so the jungle was taking its home back. The soldiers had to take it slow in the buses and beat back some of the foliage. But Reegan noted out loud that there were no vicious animals attacking us. Someone else noted after he said it that we had never been attacked by animals. The news would now spread among the people and do the work for us. It was yet another lie created by the WHO to keep us all in the dark. Even the UN had been duped.

The scenery went from luscious jungle to the scorched earth in front of the city walls. It was a welcome sight after the strenuous journey. The buses stopped in the market square, which had been cleared out to receive us. Pockets of people stood around the buildings, flanked by UN soldiers.

I saw my uncle waving frantically, held back by a UN

soldier. I jumped from my seat and ran, Borno close behind me and Reegan behind him.

My uncle stood with a group of people, but I didn't see my mother's face among them. I went straight for my uncle, leaping into his arms and nearly knocking him over. I hid my face in his shoulder as I cried.

I felt the brush of a hand on my back. It was so light, I could have ignored it. But it was also strong and solid. The smell of cinnamon and tea drifted over me. I turned my face from my uncle's shoulder and stood on my own two feet. My mother smiled and took me into her arms.

ACKNOWLEDGEMENTS

The idea for this book came to me fully formed in a dream. I have never had that happen before, and of course it took a lot of work after that to create a novel from the whispers of my brain. That work couldn't have been complete without some very important people as no writer stands alone.

First off, my amazing beta readers: Hanna, Shanthi, and Lisa. I owe you lots and lots of chocolate for your incredible work. Without you, this story wouldn't have had the emotion or the antagonism it required.

To my editor Erynn Newman, you took my story to the next level, all while keeping me laughing at your comments.

Jessica Bell, you are an incredible talent. Thank you for bringing my story to life with this amazing cover.

Albert, you gave me the space and the time to write and I can never express my gratitude. Thank you for supporting my passions and being an amazing partner to journey through life with. And in that same vein, thank you to my son Marty for being the creative and empathetic being you are. You inspire me.

I would not have gotten to this point of writing and publishing books and following my dreams without my parents and my awesome sister. Thank you!

ABOUT THE AUTHOR

Amie McCracken is an imaginist. Her stories dive deep into the what-ifs of life. Swimming in books her whole life, her career as an editor and book designer was only natural. She hails from the US of A but has lived abroad for most of her adult life. With a book or three on her nightstand, a manuscript in progress on her laptop, and a cup of tea to hand, Amie is a storyteller.

Find out more about her at amiemccrackenauthor.com.

If you liked this book, please help other readers find it by posting a review

If you would like to find out more about Amie McCracken, visit her website amiemccrackenauthor.com

If you would like to connect with Amie sign up for her newsletter at amiemccracken.com/newsletter

www.ingramcontent.com/pod-product-compliance
Lightning Source LLC
Chambersburg PA
CBHW020152310726
48970CB00006B/2113